Laurell Galindo was raised in Meridian, Texas, and graduated from Meridian I.S.D. in 2003. In 2004, she enlisted in the United States Army Reserve to serve as a Public Affairs Broadcast Specialist. She was deployed in support of Operation Iraqi Freedom from 2005 to 2006. There, she completed multiple missions to create broadcast news stories and anchored the Baghdad based program Freedom Journal Iraq for the American Forces Network. She separated honorably in 2012. Laurell is now a mother of three and resides in Texas.

Laurell Galindo

VET-ONATION

AUSTIN MACAULEY PUBLISHERS™

LONDON · CAMBRIDGE · NEW YORK · SHARJAH

Ordering Information:
Quantity sales: special discounts are available on quantity purchases by corporations, associations, and others. For details, contact the publisher at the address below.

Publisher's Cataloging-in-Publication data
Galindo, Laurell
Vet-Onation

ISBN 9781641827850 (Paperback)
ISBN 9781641827867 (Hardback)
ISBN 9781641827874 (E-Book)

The main category of the book — Fiction / Contemporary Women

www.austinmacauley.com/us

First Published (2018)
Austin Macauley Publishers LLC
40 Wall Street, 28th Floor
New York, NY 10005
USA

mail-usa@austinmacauley.com
+1 (646) 5125767

Prologue

It is awkward. It's a palm to forehead, absolutely terrible, mortifying beginning to the most incredible journey in the life of a small town, Texas girl. The cringe-worthy moment began with a well-intentioned, Texas twang, "Hey, Sugar." He was a cute Navy Petty Officer Third Class, and she was a young Army Private. They had been thrown together in a "Good Morning, Vietnam" beginning that every military broadcast journalist experiences.

It had been a long day. It seemed like zero six thirty formations, duty, schoolwork, and eighteen hundred accountability formations might get the best of Lauren. It had been almost three weeks of military occupational specialty training following nine weeks of basic training. On top of it all, she had been assigned to an Army marathon team since she'd competed in long distance running competitions in high school. That obligation required her to wake up at zero five hundred to run with the other selectees for an hour and a half before everything else. It had been exhausting. The running was voluntary, but she quickly learned when a superior requested you volunteer for anything you were really being told. Her time was not hers anymore.

Lauren was a thin, brown-haired, brown-eyed girl. With people who didn't know her, she was reserved. She knew the value of being proper and her military bearing was of the utmost importance. She was a cute girl but at the moment, a very plain one. She wore glasses and her Army uniform every day. There was never time for makeup, and her short hair was always pinned back tightly per uniform standards. She cared about her appearance but had come to realize that there was a time when she'd cared a little too much. None of it mattered now. She had too many other important things to worry about.

As she listened to the second-hand click away in her schoolhouse's editing studio, she knew she needed to be back at the Army barracks in twenty minutes for the evening accountability formation. She was running out of time and needed to finish her assignment. The innocuous ticking of the clock became louder and more deafening with every passing second. As she looked up at it in annoyance, her concentration broke. It was then she heard him quietly cursing under his breath from the next workstation. They were the lone perfectionist putting final touches on an editing assignment the others had already completed. At last, Lauren finally finished. With relief, she stood up to collect her things. She could still hear him muttering in frustration and felt kindred comfort with this obsessive-compulsiveness. She thought to herself, *Thank you, Jesus. I'm not the only one.* Lauren shoved her notebooks in her backpack and tidied her desk. She headed toward the door. It was almost time to report, and she could not be late. When Lauren reached the doorway, she stopped and turned around. She felt she should leave the room with a small reassurance. Maybe a, *"Hey, I get it. This assignment was tough for me too,"* or at the least a simple, *"I'm gone. The room is yours now."* Lauren tried to think it through in the few seconds she'd decided to be supportive. As she re-entered the room, he looked up at her, and she saw the frustration in his eyes.

Lauren hated the word lemming, but that's what she was. She did not have time for distractions. Lauren would be deploying after she graduated. She was a post 9/11 enlistee with a purpose. Soon she'd be headed halfway across the world and she was scared. He was adorable though. He needed her help, and she could spare fifteen of the twenty minutes she had left before she needed to be back at the barracks.

Lauren knew him from classroom introductions and the casual conversation they shared between lectures. He sat next to her. Davin was a tall sailor with piercing blue eyes and thinning blonde hair. His face had a unique, old soul appeal. He also had a good sense of humor, friendly smile, and he seemed like the owner of a genuinely warm heart. Davin had already spent several years in the Navy. Lauren was twenty. In fact, she had just turned twenty a few weeks before. Davin was twenty-seven and had traveled around the world on ships. She had once called them boats, which he quickly corrected. To Lauren, he was both fascinating and intimidating. She felt like a little girl playing pretend around him.

As she walked back toward him, she opened her mouth. She started to ask him if she could help. What came out of her mouth was not the flirty, colloquial Texas quip she'd intended. The words, "Hey, Sugar. Can I help?" were nowhere to be found. Instead, it was, "Hey, Snooger."

What had she just said? Her face blushed from the intensity of her embarrassment. *Why,* she thought. *I should have just left. Why did I say 'Snooger' to this man?* Lauren was cringing inside.

Davin looked down at his shoes and laughed. Lauren was sure he was embarrassed for her. It was impossible for him to keep a straight face. Of course, he was going to laugh. She would have laughed if it had been the other way around. Lauren closed her eyes and took a deep breath. She grabbed an available chair. It didn't get better though. The follow up as she sat down next to him was even worse.

"I'll rhyme," she said.

The next word out of Lauren's mouth was "Booger."

What was happening?

Davin repeated, "Hey, Snooger Booger?"

She placed her things on the floor next to her and made eye contact for the first time since this disaster began. "Apparently," she replied. Her brain, lungs, vocal cords, and face had all failed her. They both sat in awkward silence for a moment.

Then he said, "Thank you."

Chapter 1

Lauren was finally at Fort Meade, Maryland. She'd just finished basic training, and it was time to start the next leg of her journey. She would be learning her military occupational specialty as a broadcast journalist at the Defense Information School on post. August was drawing to its end, and she was glad to be in an air-conditioned classroom instead of training in the warm woods of Fort Jackson, South Carolina. She was nervous about her first day. Lauren and the other Army students reported late to the schoolhouse because their morning formation ran long. When they arrived, they selected the remaining seats located at the front of the classroom.

The instructor entered the room and stood in front of the class.

"Good morning. Today, Tuesday, August thirty-first is your first day of class, and my name is Ms. Tanya."

After sharing a brief history of her background, she continued,

"I would like each of you to now stand and introduce yourselves."

The students stood up at their workstation and took their respective turns. After everyone had finished, the instructor admonished the room.

"Every rotation, each service migrates toward its own. Since this is a multi-service military occupational specialty, some of you will need to relocate to simulate a real-world duty assignment."

Lauren had not noticed before but now realized each service had settled amongst its own. Ms. Tanya assigned, "A…B…A…B," until they all received a letter.

"Now I'd like all B's to relocate. Lauren was an A and Davin a B. She watched as he and the other B's chose new workstations around her. He walked over from where he had been sitting, pulled the seat next to hers, and sat down.

She placed her hand out toward him, "Hi. Lauren Mayer."

He replied, "Davin Hendrix."

They'd just finished introductions, but it seemed appropriate. When Davin's hand met Lauren's for a handshake, she experienced a sensation of electricity between them. It was a feeling deserving at least a silent acknowledgment. They were strangers. Lauren wasn't sure if it had been the weeks without physical contact or if there was something more there.

As the days of lectures progressed, Lauren started the practice of placing an open notebook between them every day. On this page, Davin and she would occasionally doodle or write observations about the lectures. Their friendship was progressing. Lauren also started to wonder about his personal life out of her own curiosity, but also because during this time Lauren had been assigned a battle buddy named Sandra. Sandra had taken a romantic interest in Davin as well as two others in the class. Their Drill Sergeants had ordered Lauren and Sandra to stay together at all times. They were not allowed to go anywhere without each other. Lauren quickly tired of Sandra. She was the opposite of Lauren. Sandra was the type of pretend ditsy, silly girl, Lauren could barely tolerate before, and now she was stuck with her. She was a dark-haired beauty with genetics that made her impossible to place. Sandra was a natural looker. Once while Lauren was waiting on Sandra so they could leave for the schoolhouse, she watched her apply makeup and asked,

"Why do you wear all that stuff when you don't need to?"

Sandra just laughed as if to say, "I don't know what you mean." Sandra was the type to carry cosmetics in her uniform pockets just in case she found herself in need of an emergency touch up. When Sandra flirted, which she often did, she would flutter her heavily mascaraed lashes and purse her lips as if they were naturally and permanently placed on her face in that ridiculous manner. She looked like a Jessica Rabbit wannabe.

Sandra asked Lauren questions about Davin all the time. This annoyed Lauren. She didn't have a secret window into the man's past or his everyday comings and goings. Lauren had not even dared to ask him her own curiosities. She certainly didn't want to be the go between in some elementary game of love connection. Lauren had also thought many times of the day she and Davin had shaken hands. Though she did not want to admit it, when Sandra told Lauren of her plans to ask Davin out to dinner she'd hoped that he'd see through her and turn her down. In an attempt to thwart Sandra's upcoming proposal, Lauren decided to casually mention to Davin how she was less than thrilled with her battle buddy assignment.

One day, between lectures, Lauren and Davin sat and watched as Sandra and some of the others left the room to take their break.

9

Lauren looked over at Davin and said, "She's going to drive me crazy."

He laughed, "Why?"

Her intentions of a casual mention flew out the window, and she blurted out as if she were on a therapist couch, "I'm stuck with her. She's my battle buddy. I can't go anywhere without her. She says 'like' all the time. Like is a simile. It's not a sentence filler. She flirts with everyone. Oh, by the way, she wants you bad, but that's not an exclusive crush because there are two others."

It was then Davin told her Sandra had already flirtatiously approached him.

He shared, "The other day she ordered coffee, and I was standing behind her. She turned back to me and said, 'I'll let you buy me a drink'."

Lauren laughed nervously. "Did you?"

Davin replied, "I told her, 'No, thank you.'" Relief came over Lauren. She laughed, and Davin laughed too. She was beginning to realize how much she liked him.

As the other students returned to the room, they both collected themselves for the next lecture. Ms. Tanya began, "Now we will talk about the proper and improper uses of words when speaking to an audience. Never use slang, acronyms, racial slurs, foul language, and avoid overuse of the words that and like."

On the notebook between them, Lauren wrote, "Like is a no go." She looked at Davin and smiled. He smiled back.

Chapter 2

Lauren had fallen asleep kicking herself. Why on earth had she said Snooger Booger? She awoke thinking the same thing. While she performed her early morning duties, the thought continued to haunt her. She would have to face Davin today for the first time since she'd completely embarrassed herself. They weren't supposed to socialize anyway. He was prior service and outranked her. She was a new enlistee and a private. They had inadvertently become fast friends and enjoyed talking to one another between lectures. Lauren contemplated her options as her time to report to the schoolhouse drew near. There were rules regarding fraternization. Maybe now was the time to impose them. She knew she'd miss their break time banter. As the Army students left the barracks together and headed toward the schoolhouse, Lauren's mind reeled. Her nerves became more and more unbearable with each step. She had decided she would have to ignore Davin and his yummy smile. She would most definitely have to avoid all eye contact with his beautiful blues, and she absolutely could not place the notebook between them today.

As Lauren entered the classroom, she saw Davin sitting at his workstation, watching, and waiting as if his focus had been glued to the door in anticipation of her arrival. Within her first few steps into the room, she had already done two of the three things she said she would not do. She had looked directly into his eyes and smiled to meet his smile. Her brain was still betraying her. She thought again, *Why did I say Snooger Booger?* She quietly groaned. At least she still had the notebook. Lauren pulled her things from her bag in silence and sat down. She opened her notebook. Mentally she chanted, *Do not put it between you. Do not put it between you.*

As Ms. Tanya entered the room and set up her things for the lecture, Davin leaned over and whispered, "No notebook for me today?"

Lauren looked at him in silence thinking, "Dammit!" She slid the notebook over between them. Davin had become her kryptonite. She had no power around him.

When the lecture ended, and the instructor gave permission for a break, Lauren darted to the bathroom. Usually, she and Davin would sit and talk, but today she was determined to remain silent in case her brain decided to fail her again.

Lauren gave herself a pep talk in the mirror of the empty ladies room. *"You can do this. It's no big deal. He's just a person. I'm sure he's embarrassed himself before. You got this. You can do anything. You are an American Soldier!"*

Lauren took a big breath, straightened her uniform, and fixed her hair. *God, you're crazy. You are crazy from crazy town, crazy.*

With attitude, Lauren continued, "Hi. My name is Lauren. I say Snooger Booger. So, what?"

Lauren checked her watch. Now she was really trying to waste time. She didn't want to spend any of the break sitting next to Davin. He would shatter her silence. She knew she would talk to him. She couldn't help herself. She straightened her uniform again. *Okay, time to quit talking to yourself. You can't let him make you crazy like this.*

She took another deep breath. It was a good thing she'd stopped when she did because someone had just pushed the door open to enter the bathroom. Lauren turned, said hello, and exited confidently.

Lauren strode into the classroom prepared, but when she got there, Davin was not sitting at his workstation. She paused, looked around the room perplexed, and sat down to wait for Ms. Tanya. The lecture was about to start again. Lauren looked at the notes and doodles from the last few weeks in the notebook. She smiled to herself. She knew she was fighting a losing battle. She did like Davin more than she wanted to admit. He had not even mentioned the evening before. She was sure he was kind. As she continued to stare Lauren heard a familiar flirty laugh. It was Sandra approaching the classroom. Lauren thought, *She is so obnoxious when she flirts.* She wondered which fly had landed in Sandra's web of seduction and watched the door for the revealing entrance. She was shocked when Sandra and Davin walked through the door together. He couldn't possibly have fallen for it? Could he? Lauren's eyes followed Davin as he parted from Sandra and crossed the room toward her. Lauren didn't know if she even blinked. As he stood above her, he looked at Lauren and smiled.

She looked at him puzzled. Davin sat down, leaned toward her, and whispered, "You'll have to talk to me to find out." With that, the lecture began.

Lauren couldn't concentrate. Davin did not seem like the kind of person who would be attracted to someone like Sandra. *What do I know about men,* thought Lauren. Lauren and Sandra were both young. Sandra was beautiful. Maybe he was the typical port call sailor. Lauren hardly knew anything about him anyway. She was disappointed. Once she'd pinpointed this feeling, she wondered why she cared. Davin was allowed to like whomever he pleased. Then Lauren remembered the handshake. There was something there. She started to get upset with him. She thought, *He's so stupid if he falls for her mess.* Her mind was jumping all over the emotional map. *I hate feelings. I'm not here for distractions anyway. Shut it down,* she silently instructed. Lauren decided she would not be talking to Davin anymore. She had obviously been a terrible judge of character.

"Okay, we will break for lunch. Be back in one hour," said Ms. Tanya. Lauren's mind raced back to reality. She quickly gathered her things to meet Sandra. After all, they were not allowed to go anywhere without each other.

Davin reached for Lauren's arm and said, "I need to talk to you." There it was again. Lauren felt the electric, instant goose bumps thing. She had never experienced anything like it before. She paused to feel its full effect.

After a brief moment, she impatiently said, "I can't. I have to go." Lauren was irritated she'd let him get to her, and now he'd broken her silence with one touch.

Lauren raced out the door of the classroom to find Sandra. When she reached her, they set off to the Army chow hall. There were two chow halls on campus to accommodate all of the students and staff members. They weren't assigned to one branch or another, however, over time one was deemed the Army's and the other the Navy's. All other branches fell in wherever they felt comfortable. The Navy students were seldom seen eating with the Army students. It was a strange segregation Lauren had yet to get used to.

On the way, Sandra announced with excitement, "Hey, I have good news. I have a date. Well, we have a date with Davin this weekend."

"We have a date," asked Lauren.

"Yeah, I asked him if he wanted to do something this weekend and he said yes. He has a car you know."

Lauren did not know this. It was typical from what she knew of Sandra though. There was always an ulterior motive. It seemed flirting to get what she wanted was a game she had mastered long ago because she was good at it. Lauren had to give the she-devil her due.

"Wow. Okay," said Lauren. She didn't know what to think anymore. As they reached the chow hall and stood in line, Sandra continued to tell her all the details of her conversation with Davin. Lauren was in shock. The last thing she wanted to do was to babysit a date for someone she constantly wanted to roll her eyes at and the man who gave her magic moments with one touch. Lauren put her back to the wall. She leaned against it as she stood in the slow-moving line occasionally adding an 'uh-huh' to make it appear she was still listening. She looked back toward the end of the line and saw him. Davin was waiting. He had followed them to the Army chow hall.

Lauren interrupted Sandra, "Your boy toy is here." She pointed him out to her, and Sandra seemed pleased.

Lauren and Sandra reached the front of the line, selected their meals, and sat down to eat. Lauren realized she'd forgotten silverware and excused herself. Davin was choosing his own eating utensils.

As they stood, side by side, Lauren said, "I heard the good news."

Davin replied, "I wanted to talk to you, but you've been ignoring me all morning."

"Well I'm listening now," she retorted.

"She asked me. I said yes because I knew you wouldn't ask me and you'd have to go with her anyway."

She suddenly realized this was true. Sandra would've never agreed to accompany Lauren and Davin. She was too self-involved. The other way around was better for everyone.

Lauren needed time to think about it all. Her tough demeanor softened, "I'll talk to you in class."

"Yes," said Davin. "See you in class. We can talk more there."

Lauren returned to sit with Sandra. "What did he say," she asked.

Lauren replied, "He wanted to make sure I was okay with the date stuff since you and I are battle buddies and I'll have to go."

It was Saturday. Davin and Lauren had discussed all the possibilities for the day earlier that week. They had settled on the National Aquarium at the Inner Harbor in Baltimore. When Sandra asked where they'd be going, Lauren told her. It seemed everyone was a fan of the Aquarium. As Sandra and Lauren waited outside the barracks for Davin to pick them up, Lauren started to feel bad. She was uncomfortable with the whole idea.

All remorse quickly dissipated when Sandra said, "I have another date at the mall tomorrow with a Marine! You don't mind, do you? You'll have to come with me there too."

Lauren smiled, "Seriously?"

"Yes, but I don't want you to hang around for that one. It's the mall. You can find something to do, right?"

Lauren laughed, "I guess. Malls have shoe stores, right? I'll be fine."

Davin pulled up, and Lauren got in the back while Sandra helped herself to the passenger seat. Sandra talked non-stop during the ride to the aquarium. Lauren sat quietly in the backseat, grinning happily and taking in the scenery. She sensed eyes on her and broke her gaze to catch Davin glancing at her in his rearview mirror. Today her time would be hers, and she couldn't wait to enjoy it. When they arrived, Davin and Lauren quickly exited the car only to find themselves waiting on Sandra as she lingered inside to touch up her makeup in the visor mirror. Lauren made eye contact with Davin, laughed, and motioned her head in Sandra's direction.

He asked, "Why are you laughing?"

Lauren replied, "You'd better make this a memorable date. She's got another one tomorrow with a Marine."

Sandra exited the car without hearing their exchange. She inquired, "Are we ready?"

Lauren sarcastically answered, "Yes. We're just waiting on you, beauty queen."

Lauren was excited. She tagged along behind Davin and Sandra most of the day. He had concocted the silly idea, so it was his to pay for. Sandra was her usual self, and Davin was noticeably distracted. Lauren loved every second of it and had an excellent view from the rear. The best part of the aquarium came when Lauren spotted an exhibit about whales and the way they communicate with each other. She walked ahead to take it in. On the wall, there was a box with several buttons. Each played a different recording of a whale sound. The goal was to listen and then try to vocally simulate the noise to see how well you could match the pitch. The closer the recording and simulation were the more points were shown on a screen. This was right up Lauren's alley. She pushed the first button. As Davin and Sandra approached, the first recording finished playing. It was Lauren's turn to simulate the noise, and she did without hesitation.

Sandra insisted, "Stop it. You're embarrassing."

Lauren thought about it. It should have been embarrassing. Davin was standing right there, but it wasn't. She had already made a fool of herself once, and he was kind.

She pushed the next button, and a new whale sound rang out. A voice from the box said, "It's your turn now." Again, Lauren very seriously simulated with all the gusto her diaphragm, lungs, and vocal cords could muster. She looked over at Davin as she finished. He was laughing so hard she thought he might cry.

Lauren saw her score. "Look. That time was good. It was better than the first one. You should try Sandra. It's fun."

Sandra sneeringly said, "No, thank you. I'll just take pictures."

Lauren looked at Davin. He walked over and stood next to her. "You pick the next one, Davin."

He did. Lauren and Davin were obviously meant for this type of stuff. Their combined effort produced a simulated whale duet for the record books.

Sandra had enough. "I'm going to the restroom," she said before abruptly walking away. Lauren and Davin were laughing so hard that tears filled their eyes.

As they found a place to sit and wait for Sandra, Davin confessed, "I like you so much, Lauren. There's something about you. I wish it were just the two of us today."

Lauren stopped laughing, "Are you really, really, really sure we're not all here because you were excited to take Sandra out and are now having buyer's remorse?"

He reassured her, "No. I wish you wouldn't have left us alone so much."

She smiled. Lauren wished it had just been the two of them too.

Lauren and Davin were so focused on each other they did not notice Sandra had returned. She interrupted, "Can we get something to eat? I'm hungry."

Davin said, "Sure." They all exited the aquarium and wandered over to the Harbor Place and Gallery snapping pictures of each other along the way. While Davin and Sandra selected a restaurant, Lauren spotted a hat in a boutique window display she could not resist. It was a bright red crab with two large crossed eyes, which protruded from the center of the hat with the assistance of pipe cleaners. On the left and right sides respectively was a claw followed by three legs designed in the same bendable fashion.

Lauren had to have one. She went into the boutique without interrupting Davin and Sandra to let them know where she was going. Lauren purchased the hat and placed it on her head. She then returned to find Davin and Sandra who were still debating.

Sandra looked over at her and rolled her eyes. "Why?"

"Why not," replied Lauren.

Sandra continued, "I'm never taking you anywhere again."

"Ha," said Lauren. "I'm your battle buddy. You're stuck with me until we phase up."

Sandra was not amused, "Well, thank God that's next week." Lauren laughed.

Davin then interjected, "You guys don't have to do this anymore after next week?"

Lauren explained, "It's a transitional phase thing. We'll have been here long enough next week for our Drill Sergeants to trust us on our own."

Lauren was sure he wished she'd told him about this before, but it had not come up. Besides, he was the one who'd accepted Sandra's proposal. Lauren wasn't sorry. She was glad to be away from the base. At last, Davin and Sandra reached a decision. The three ate and reminisced about their day before returning to Fort Meade. Lauren could tell Sandra had lost interest in Davin by the time they all said their goodbyes. Sandra jumped out, tapped the side of the car twice and said, "thank you" through the open window. Then she sprinted toward the barracks.

Lauren exited more calmly, "Really, thank you. I had a lot of fun."

As she walked away, Davin asked, "Hey, Lauren. Do you want to exchange numbers?"

Lauren turned around and answered, "Yeah, I think I'd like that."

It was Sunday. The only day the Army students were allowed to sleep in if they didn't have duty. Lauren had been sound asleep when Sandra who did have duty burst into her room with a flashlight. She was doing her morning count of soldiers on the female floor.

Sandra was wide-awake and singing obnoxiously, "Today is my date with the Marine!" She shined the bright light on Lauren's face. She continued singing. "He's cute. He's cuter than Davin. I don't know what I was thinking. You can have him. You're welcome. Oh, don't forget you have to come with me, but not come with me." She paused from her made up melody and loudly said, "Wink, wink!"

Lauren was half-asleep and trying to make sense of Sandra's heavily caffeinated ramblings. Lauren looked at her alarm clock. "It's zero five thirty. What is wrong with you? I get to sleep in."

Sandra replied, "You are sleeping in. You're usually up at zero five hundred for that marathon thingy. When is that anyway?"

Lauren yelled, "Next Saturday. Now go away before I beat you with this pillow."

Sandra continued, "Like a pillow fight?"

Lauren asked, "What are you on? I need some of that next week."

Sandra turned off her flashlight and stepped out into the hall announcing loudly, "Room 312; Accounted for!"

Lauren prayed, "Dear God, why on earth did you give me a bat shit crazy battle. Heaven help me." She then rolled over, yawned, and fell back to sleep.

When Lauren awoke, she dressed and went down to the study room of the barracks. Lauren didn't feel like studying, but needed to. There was always so much going on at the barracks during the weekend, and she was having a hard time thinking of anything other than Davin. Lauren left the study room to look for Sandra, but she was nowhere to be found. Lauren thought she might still be awake judging from the hyperactive encounter they had earlier. She was tempted to call Davin but thought better of it. He was exactly the kind of distraction she did not need. She needed to focus. Lauren went back to the study room. She concentrated successfully for a bit before her mind circled back to him. *This is impossible right now,* Lauren thought. What she needed was a walk to clear her head. Lauren closed her books and headed up the stairs to return them to her room. As she reached the top floor, she saw Sandra enter the bathroom.

Lauren headed for the bathroom and found her waiting in line for the shower. "Sandra, what time are we leaving for your thing? I'd like to get out of here," she said.

Sandra ordered, "Be ready in an hour." Lauren sarcastically saluted in acknowledgment and headed back to her room to change.

An hour later, Sandra knocked on and then opened the door to Lauren's room where she'd been waiting, "Let's go. The taxi will be here in five."

Lauren grabbed her wallet, and they headed to the usual pickup location. As they walked Sandra asked, "Did you talk to Davin today?"

Lauren replied, "No."

Sandra continued, "Why not? I gave him to you." Lauren was getting tired of Sandra's notion that she could gift a human being, but she let it go. She was done with this conversation and relieved the taxi had arrived like an angel of mercy to rescue her from it.

"Perfect," said Sandra. They both got in and left for the mall.

When they arrived at the mall, Sandra told Lauren the plan. They agreed to meet back at the same spot in a few hours. Sandra set off to find her Marine and Lauren watched her walk away wondering which direction the nearest shoe store was. Lauren loved shoes. She quickly located a mall map. As she stared at it trying to pinpoint her current location, her phone rang.

She answered it without looking away, "Hello."

She immediately recognized the voice on the other end. "Hi. It's Davin. How's Sandra's date going?"

Lauren laughed, "I wouldn't know. I'm by myself. Hey, do you know this place? I'm at the mall. Where's the nearest shoe store?"

She continued to search the map, "Never mind, I found it!

Davin laughed at her enthusiasm and said, "I can meet you there if you'd like?"

Lauren questioned, "You want to go shoe shopping with me?"

Davin answered unconvincingly, "Yeah, I guess. I can be there in fifteen minutes."

Lauren was surprised he even offered. "Okay," she said. Before she could add anything else, he hung up. Lauren pulled the phone away from her face and looked at it. She smiled. She had been smiling a lot lately.

When Davin arrived, he found Lauren sitting on the floor of the shoe store surrounded by several boxes of high heels. Lauren looked up at him. She was pleased he had called and driven to the mall to keep her company.

Without even a hello she said, "They're all so pretty. Choosing a pair is hard. Help me." Davin let her model several of them and helped her settle on a pair of shimmery brown pumps. They had an intricate cut-out flower detail with mesh embellishments on the pointed toes. They were stunning. "Okay, now I have to put the rest of these away," she said.

Lauren handed Davin the box of shoes they'd selected and began to pack up and re-shelve the rest. She was falling quickly for this man. He was full of surprises. As she placed the last box back on the shelf, she glanced in the direction where she'd left him, but he was no longer there. She scanned the room. It took her a moment to find him, but she spotted him. Davin had walked to the payment counter and was buying her shoes. Lauren watched as he exchanged, what she assumed were pleasantries, with the cashier. They were too far for her to hear their conversation. She continued to spectate in awe as he walked back toward her.

When he reached her, box in hand, he said, "I meant to purchase them before you finished picking up your mess."

Lauren stepped on the end of his sentence, "Are you going to be my Prince Charming?"

He replied using the same words she'd said the day before. "Yeah, I think I'd like that."

Chapter 3

Lauren felt like she was on a cloud. Davin had come into her life unexpectedly. She was scared and intimidated by the new military adventure she'd embarked upon, but with Davin's positive reassurance she'd found her stride. Lauren hoped no one would notice how fond of him she'd become. Ms. Tanya did though. One day between lectures, she pulled them both into her office. "Private Mayer. Petty Officer Hendrix. Come with me please."

Both Davin and Lauren followed her to a room where they all sat down. She began sharply, "Petty Officer Hendrix, you know better. You are prior service, and you know the rules about fraternizing with new enlistees. Private Mayer, I have seen these schoolhouse romances crash and burn repeatedly. Hendrix, you'd better think long and hard about your intentions and how they are affecting this girl. It's best you both end this nonsense immediately. Now, go!"

Lauren and Davin stood up and left her office. They were both in shock. Aside from the occasional notes in the notebook and the break time banter, they had not been disruptive of the lectures or neglectful of their studies. They had maybe flirted a little more than they should of, but they certainly hadn't done anything wrong. Lauren's anger mounted the more she replayed what happened.

She stopped in the hall and looked at Davin. "What the hell was that," she asked.

Lauren was angry and sarcastically quipped, "I chaperoned your date with Sandra." She was in denial. Lauren did not want to concede she might have let the flirtation get away from her.

She continued, "We haven't been inappropriate. We haven't even discussed romance."

Davin swore, "I have no idea, Lauren. I'm sorry. I can't believe she called us in there and spoke to us like that."

Lauren stomped away. She was furious. She felt like crying, and she wasn't going to break down in front of Davin or anyone else.

The rest of the week Lauren was cautious. She did not want to be associated with any impropriety. Lauren hardly spoke to Davin. She missed him so much even though he was sitting right next to her. There were several things she wanted to share with him. She hadn't realized how much of a friend he'd become. He was her best friend. They could talk, laugh, and joke about anything.

As Friday approached Davin asked, "Hey, are you still phasing up? I'd like to take you out. We can talk about what happened earlier this week."

Lauren couldn't. She and her team would be running at the Baltimore Marathon on Saturday morning. That Friday the runners and Drill Sergeants would all be eating dinner together to go over last-minute details. "I can't. I have a marathon thing this weekend. I need to pick up some items from the Post Exchange this evening. If you want to accompany me, I'll meet you at the bus stop at nineteen hundred hours," she said. Davin happily agreed to meet her.

Davin met Lauren as planned. As they waited for the bus, Lauren said, "I don't understand why Ms. Tanya made assumptions and then admonished us. She should have at least asked us the nature of our relationship. Don't you think?"

Davin agreed, "Yeah, that was weird." The bus pulled up, and they boarded. It was a short ride to the PX from the barracks.

Lauren shared some of the most recent shenanigans from the Army barracks. "The other day some idiots on the male floor pulled the fire alarm in the middle of the night in honor of someone's birthday. We all had to evacuate. The Drill Sergeants were angry. Everyone had to do push-ups for twenty minutes while the fire department cleared the building."

Davin thought this was hilarious. "Oh, then a couple of Air Force guys came over and stole our barrack's flag. So, the Army guys retaliated by sneaking into their building. They tied up the airman on duty, reclaimed our flag, and seized theirs." The bus arrived at their destination. Lauren and Davin got off and entered the PX. There was so much to tell him.

As Davin followed her through the store, he also shared. "I filled out my wish list for my next duty assignment. I requested Rota, Spain. I've got my fingers crossed. It's supposed to be awesome there," he said. The week's events might as well have been a lifetime to catch up on. Lauren finished up her shopping trip, paid for her things, and they both exited the store just as the bus was pulling up.

Davin stepped aside and stated, "Ladies first."

"Thank you, kind stranger," replied Lauren. They picked two seats together and sat down. Lauren sat closest to the window.

As she gazed out pondering what a lovely time they'd had, Davin leaned in close. "Lauren, I want to kiss you," he confessed. The sound of his voice so close to her took her breath away. He hadn't even touched her this time. Lauren could hardly stand the tingling sensation washing over her. She could feel the goose bumps crawling down her body.

Lauren turned to face him. "Davin, now is not the time, and this is not the place."

"I know, but I want to. I want you to know I want to," he said. If Ms. Tanya took issue with the innocent flirtation of their friendship in class, she would most definitely take issue with a bus make-out session. At that moment, Lauren was overwhelmed with the urge to kiss him too. Instead, she took his hand and squeezed it tight. They stared intently into each other's eyes as the bus came to a stop. The ride back had been the shortest Lauren could remember. They stood, exited the bus, and waited silently for it to pull away.

When the bus had gone, Davin drew her close and hugged her tight. "Think about it," he requested. Lauren could feel him becoming erect against her.

She sank into his arms and responded, "How could I not."

The next day Lauren was filled with butterflies. She could not stop thinking about Davin or her growing desire to kiss his yummy mouth. She was also nervous about Ms. Tanya and keeping her composure in class, dinner with her Drill Sergeants, and Saturday's running event. The day passed with ease. Davin had asked if she wanted him to attend the marathon for support. Lauren told him not to worry about it. The only difficulty came when she tried to close her eyes that night.

She turned on some music and struggled to fall asleep. As she lay there, one song ended and a new one began. The singer belted the refrain. Lauren had heard the song many times, but tonight it had new meaning. She paused her thoughts and listened. It was as if the tune was personally urging her to indulge in her feelings for Davin.

Lauren sat up and snatched her phone from her nightstand.

She hesitated but dialed anyway. "Hello," he answered.

"Sorry, it's late. I can't sleep," she said.

He reassured her, "No. It's fine. I like hearing your voice. You need to rest though. You've got a big day tomorrow."

She agreed, "Yeah. I know. I've been thinking about us."

Davin answered, "You have? I meant it, Lauren."

Lauren continued, "I want you to know I want you to kiss me too."

"That's great news," he said with a chuckle. "Let me take you out tomorrow when you get back from the race. I'll take you somewhere special."

Lauren agreed. They said their goodnights and hung up. It seemed Ms. Tanya's well-intentioned intervention had only pushed them further into each other's arms. Lauren was able to fall asleep peacefully knowing she had given into her feelings and confessed a little of her heart.

It was the day of the race, and Lauren was excited. She and her team members had put in countless early morning hours running the base in preparation. Lauren could not wait to hit the pavement. She was the first leg of her four-man team. The starting pistol fired, and she left the line with the hundreds of others who were eager to commence the race. Lauren knew she had told Davin not to worry about coming, but as she ran through the streets of Baltimore, she still looked for him. No energy drink or caffeinated beverage could ever compare to the motivation she felt to finish this part of her day so she could see Davin later. Lauren finished her six and a half miles in just under forty-five minutes. She handed off the tracking device she'd been given to her waiting teammate. She was relieved her part was over. As she walked back toward the staging area around the finish line, she hoped her teammates would complete their portions of the relay just as quickly. While Lauren waited, she realized she was tired. She thought, *If I'm this tired now, I'll be exhausted later.* She hoped it would not be the case, but as time passed, she felt even worse. Lauren was ready to find her bed and her pillow when she finally spotted the last runner on her team as he approached the finish line. She cheered him across. There were so many people standing around. Lauren had not located her other two teammates until then. All four were reunited for the first time in hours. They congratulated one another and shared stories from each of their experiences while they waited to collect their medals and return to the base. Lauren was more than ready to leave when the group decided it was time to go.

Upon arriving back at Fort Meade, Lauren called Davin to cancel. She'd barely been able to keep her eyes open on the ride back.

He answered, "Hey Lauren. I'm so excited about tonight. I made a reservation for dinner. I thought we could see a movie too. I'll pick you up at eighteen hundred?"

Dammit, she thought. Lauren did not have the heart to tell him she was too tired.

She confirmed, "I'll be ready. You can pick me up outside the barracks."

Lauren slowly made it up the stairs to her room. She opened her door and looked at her bed. It looked inviting, but Davin's voice was inviting too. Lauren opened her drawers. She did not have many civilian clothes. Uniforms had taken over her life. Before today, she hadn't had a lot of need for everyday garments anyway. Lauren had just phased up. The Drill Sergeants had also given her an overnight pass from the barracks because she and her team had done well at the marathon. Lauren had not intended to use it. She desperately wanted to crawl into her bed. Instead, she selected a pair of sage corduroy hip huggers and a matching jacket. She grabbed a white tank top for underneath. Lauren stopped when she reached her underwear drawer. In amongst all her tighty-whities and sports bras was a lovely taupe lace bra with matching underwear. She had not worn them before. Lauren pulled them out and tossed them on top of her pile. Then she gathered her clothing, towel, and shower items and headed to the bathroom. Lauren quickly showered, dressed, fixed her hair, and put on makeup.

She looked at herself in the mirror. For a moment she didn't recognize herself. *"Damn, you clean up good,"* she said. Giving herself pep-talks in the mirror was something Lauren had done since she was a little girl. With that, she went back to her room to hang up her towel and put her things away. Lauren grabbed her phone and looked at the time. Realizing she was running behind, she quickly grabbed her purse and headed down the stairs to meet Davin.

As she exited the barracks, she saw Davin waiting for her in his vehicle. He was watching her walk toward him. It seemed like the longest most awkward walk of her life.

Lauren got in and buckled her seat belt. "Sorry. Have you been waiting long?" she asked.

Davin replied, "Wow." He paused to take her in. "You are beautiful."

Lauren retorted, "I'm tired, but thank you." They pulled away and headed out for the evening.

A few minutes later they arrived at what appeared to be a Mexican restaurant. "Mexican," she asked.

"Well, I thought since you've been away from Texas for so long you might like a taste of home. I bet they even have tequila!" Davin impressed Lauren with his thoughtfulness. She would have to tell him she wasn't old enough to drink alcohol, but at least she could eat something akin to Tex-Mex.

They entered the restaurant. The server seated them and asked, "What can I get you to drink?" Davin ordered a bottled beer.

When it was Lauren's turn she said, "I'll have water, no lemon, please." The server left to get their drinks. Under the table, Davin placed his hand on Lauren's thigh. Again, she felt the familiar sensation which she'd come to find comforting.

He asked, "Why didn't you order a drink?"

Lauren started to make up an excuse but decided now was as good a time as any to tell him. "Water is a drink. Also, I feel dehydrated from earlier, but really, I am only twenty. I turned twenty a few weeks ago." She smiled at Davin uneasily. Lauren watched his face as he processed the information.

He questioned, "Are you serious?"

She laughed nervously and joked, "Man, I wish I had a drink now. Yes, I'm serious."

Lauren pulled her license from the wallet in her purse and handed it to him. "Here's my license," she said.

As he examined her card, the server arrived with their drinks. Lauren requested, "Will you excuse me? I need to visit the ladies room." She thought they could both use a moment.

Lauren took her time. She wondered how old Davin had thought she was. Lauren made her way back to the table. Once reseated, Davin handed Lauren her license back. "I figured you left me here," he said.

She responded, "You're my ride." They both laughed.

Davin explained, "I was caught off-guard. I don't care how old you are. There's something special about you. Sometimes you'll sigh in class, and the sound sends shivers down my spine. I like you, Lauren." Lauren could relate. The server arrived at the table with a margarita and asked if they were ready.

Lauren and Davin placed their dinner order. When she left, Davin slid the cocktail over to her. "You are going to enjoy your meal even if we have to be creative to get you a drink," he said. Lauren wondered how she'd gotten so lucky. As they ate, they talked. There was never a boring moment or lull in their conversation despite Lauren's increasing fatigue. The cocktail had not helped matters either. When the server came to check on them once more, Lauren asked if they could get the check. Davin insisted on paying the bill, and they left the restaurant.

As they walked toward the car, Davin asked, "Do you have a movie in mind?" Lauren knew she would definitely fall asleep in the darkness of a theater.

She sighed, "I can't, Davin. I'm exhausted. There's no way I would make it through a movie without passing out on you. It's a shame because I was given an overnight pass to enjoy, and…"

Davin interrupted her, "Wait. You have an overnight pass?"

Lauren responded cautiously, "Yes."

Eager to share a proposal, Davin continued, "I have an idea. I'll take you back to your noisy barracks and your awful Army mattress if you want or I can drive you to a world of feather down comfort, bathtubs, and room service."

Lauren thought this sounded like a cunning ploy. She trusted him though and said, "Under any other circumstances and with any other man that would be a hard no. You just dangled my kind of heaven." Lauren felt like a horse and Davin had the carrot.

He opened her door, and she got in. She watched as he quickly crossed in front of the car and opened his door. "Well," he asked as he got into the car and put the key in the ignition.

After thinking a moment, Lauren inquired, "Two beds?"

Davin repeated with a smile, "Two beds."

Lauren took a deep breath and sighed, "Okay, take me to paradise."

On the way to the hotel, Lauren asked, "How do you know about this place?"

Davin told her, "I've been researching activities we could do and places I could take you to impress you. I've been planning all sorts of things. I was hoping you liked me as much as I liked you."

Lauren was quite the smitten kitten. When they arrived, Davin took care of everything while Lauren wandered around the lobby taking in its artful decor. Davin called to her, "Ready?" Lauren walked toward him and took his hand. She was both excited and nervous. These feelings quickly turned to concern when she resurfaced from her enamored haze to realize she only had the things she was wearing. Davin led her through the hotel to their room, he opened the door, and they went in. It was stunning.

As Lauren familiarized herself, Davin said, "See, two beds."

She laughed, "And Champaign." Lauren pointed to a bottle chilling in an ice bucket next to two Champaign flutes on a table in the room. It was everything Davin had promised, bathtub included.

Lauren fell forward onto the fluff of one of the beds announcing, "This one's mine." She heard a cork pop and rolled to her side. As Davin poured the Champaign, Lauren addressed her dilemma. "I can't sleep in these clothes. Is that okay with you?"

Davin smiled and said, "I won't peek if you don't want me too."

Lauren countered with a snicker, "Yeah, right."

Davin handed her a flute and sat on the bed across from hers. They chatted until both had finished their first glass. Davin poured them another. Lauren could not believe how quickly the bubbles were going to her head. She was tired, and all her inhibitions were fading fast. She stood up, handed her glass to Davin, and walked to the end of the bed. Lauren unbuttoned her pants. She kicked them off clumsily.

"What are you doing," he asked.

"I'm getting ready for bed," she responded. She pulled off her jacket and threw it on top of her newly started pile. Lauren then pulled her tank top awkwardly over her head and tossed it too. Standing in her taupe lace bra and panties, she threw her head back laughing.

She put her hands in the air and said, "Let me introduce you to Amazing Grace!" Still amused she took a bow. When she stood back up, she looked at Davin with his kind eyes and yummy smile.

He was looking at her as if she were the most remarkable beauty he'd ever seen. "Lauren, you look like a supermodel." Lauren liked this complement. She nodded her head in agreement. Following basic training and marathon preparation, she was in the best shape of her life.

"It's all the running," she said. Davin stood up, sat both Champaign glasses down, and walked toward her. He grabbed her hand, led her back to her bed, pulled back the covers, and laid her down. He then tucked her in and kissed her on the forehead. Lauren couldn't help herself anymore. She was hopelessly in love with the man.

She pointed and said, "You don't have to sleep in that bed."

Davin knelt down beside her and asked, "Are you sure?"

"I want to be a little spoon. Your little spoon," she said. Lauren then began to take off her underwear beneath the covers. "This bed is wonderful and I feel wonderful."

Davin asked, "What are you doing now?"

Lauren replied, "I'm taking off my undies and then I'm taking a nap." It was almost twenty-two hundred hours.

Davin questioned, "A nap? Lauren, it's late."

"I know," she said.

"I'm taking a naked nap. I will be enjoying that bathtub sometime soon. You can take a naked nap with me or not. I don't care."

Lauren knew she was being flirtatiously rotten. She watched with a grin as Davin began to undress in front of her. His body was lean and well-built, but not overly muscular.

She thought he was a stunning specimen. She whined, "Oh my God. Everything about you is yummy." Davin smiled and continued to undress. As he removed his underwear, her eyes met his erect penis with uneasiness. He was intimidatingly large. Lauren had only ever seen one other man naked. In comparison, Davin's physique was far more impressive. She noted a birthmark located near his shaft.

Lauren silently reassured herself, "Anything with a beauty mark is not going to hurt me."

He crawled into bed and wrapped his strong arms around her. Lauren closed her eyes.

As her skin melted into his, she asked, "Can we just sleep?"

He kissed the crown of her head and said, "Yes, but first will you do something for me?"

Lauren opened her eyes. She was not ready to be intimate with him. She was still processing the size of his manhood. Lauren turned slightly to look at him.

He whispered, "Will you call me what you called me in the editing studio the other day?"

Lauren giggled, "Snooger Booger?"

Davin replied, "Yeah, but say it like you mean it."

Lauren laughed harder and then whispered, "Okay? Goodnight, Shnuga Booga."

Davin sighed, "Yup, that's it. I'm your Shnuga Booga. Goodnight, Lauren." She nuzzled into him further and fell fast asleep.

Lauren awoke blissfully around midnight. In her stillness, she could feel the rhythm of Davin's heart and hear the cadence of his breath against her skin. She could not imagine anything more soothing. He had held her close the entire time. Lauren beamed in the darkness musing about the many conversations and moments they had shared. She was incredibly happy. She did not want to stir from his embrace, but could not help satisfy another craving coming over her. It had been months since Lauren soaked in a bathtub. Her military life was full of lines and community showers. Privacy was a limited and coveted novelty. She gently tried to sneak from his embrace. Lauren was almost free when Davin awoke.

"Where are you going?" he asked.

"I'm going to run myself a bath," she said.

"Alright, I'll be right here when you're done," he replied. Still naked, Lauren found the bathroom in the dark and turned on the light. She quietly shut the door and adjusted the water to an inviting temperature. She had just slipped in, turned on the timer, and sat back in the jet of bubbles when Davin opened the door and poked his head in.

"Do you mind if I join you?"

Although Lauren had looked forward to solitude, she had come to accept she could not tell him no. "I suppose," she said.

Davin stepped into the bathroom with their flutes from before filled with the remaining bubbly. "This is it. We killed the bottle," he informed her. Lauren smirked and held her hands out to take the glasses so Davin could get in. They sipped the last of the Champagne enjoying the warmth of the water and the bubbles stirring around them.

Davin reached for Lauren's face. He looked deeply into her eyes and confessed, "Lauren, I'm in love with you."

Lauren, overcome with emotion, began to well up with tears. "Oh, Lauren, please don't cry."

Lauren replied, "No. I'm not upset. I'm in love with you too. I didn't mean to be, but I am."

Lauren was terrible when it came to dealing with emotions. She was always one to keep her cards close to her chest, and now here she was showing them to Davin and crying about it. Davin continued, "You and I could have such a wonderful life together if that's what we want." Lauren listened intently to her handsome man and his beautiful words. "You are perfect, Lauren. There isn't a single hair or freckle I'd change about you. I've never met anyone like you in my life. I know I never will again because God broke the mold when he made you and gifted you with your heart and mind. Your soul speaks to me. I don't know how to explain it. I've never had anything like this happen before. I see you. I see who you truly are. My heart melts over and over again knowing we were made for each other; knowing that the best days of our lives haven't come yet." Lauren was crying by the time he finished.

She conceded, "I knew we had something special from our first handshake. Even though we were meeting for the first time, I felt like I'd known you my whole life." Lauren sniffled and shared, "I hate snot."

Davin chuckled and wiped a tear from her cheek. Slowly, they each leaned toward each other and finally exchanged the sexually charged, passionate kiss they'd been longing for. Suddenly the bathtub timer clicked, and the water around them calmed. When they ended their kiss, Lauren sat back. She was completely relaxed. Reclining in the still of the tub, debating their next move, Lauren made some ripples of her own. She had not meant to, but unexpectedly in the space between them rose a handful of bubbles to the surface. Davin, realizing what had happened, began to laugh hysterically. Lauren was mortified.

She grinned in embarrassment and pointed at Davin. "This is your fault. I guess Champagne gives me gas?" She urged, "Stop laughing. I was relaxed!" Davin attempted to compose himself. Lauren watched as he exited the tub and wrapped a towel around his waist.

He pulled a towel for her from the shelf and held it out. "Come here," he said. Lauren stood up, exited the tub, and stepped into his arms and the waiting towel. As he wrapped it around her, he said, "There is not a single thing I'd change about you. Let's go back to bed."

Lauren and Davin crawled back under the covers. Davin kissed her passionately while positioning himself between her legs. Lauren's body responded to his every cue. She became increasingly wet with her desire for his body. Davin slowly and purposefully moved from her lips down her neck to her breasts where he lingered. He lovingly caressed the right one with his tongue while he passed his callous palm over her left. Her exposed nipple became erect in response to his touch. He then switched sides performing the same loving gesture. When he was satisfied, he proceeded to her stomach and down further until he finally reached his intended destination.

As he kissed her tenderly, Lauren suddenly became uneasy. She sat up a bit and breathlessly called out to him, "Davin, I'm sorry. Um, could you please not do that down there?" Lauren was nervous.

Davin stopped, looked up at her, and ran his fingers back and forth over her hipbone while he spoke, "Lauren if you don't want me to, I won't. I love you. I love every part of you. I want to taste you. Please, let me taste you?"

Lauren laid back. "Okay." She had never had a man treat her to such an exquisite encounter. The more he kissed and danced his tongue over her the more she ached for him. Lauren groaned in pleasure until the stimulation was too much to bear. "Davin, can I please have you? I want you inside me. Please," she begged.

Davin worked his way back kissing her body along the way. Before he entered her, he stopped to ask, "Lauren, are you sure? I want this to be special."

Lauren kissed him, "Yes, I'm sure. I feel special."

With that, Davin complied with her request and entered her slowly. Lauren felt as though he filled every bit of her up as he stroked her tenderly. The rhythm of his deliberate thrusting consumed Lauren. The sensation gradually became more and more intense until she was on the verge of climax. She paused from her groans of delight. "I'm cumming, man of mine."

He responded, "Me too." As her muscles tighten around him, she could feel the pulsing of his release. He held her tight and buried his head in her neck. In the calm of their exhaustion, she felt him pulse twice more inside of her. It was over. They had made love to each other for the first time, and it had been amazing.

Lauren took a deep breath and with a sigh whispered, "Just stay." Davin kissed her cheek and closed his eyes. Together they fell asleep locked in a gentle intimate and physical embrace.

Chapter 4

As the next weeks passed, Lauren and Davin should have been solely focused on their studies and upcoming graduation. However, their affections for each other were consuming. They spent every lecture break, meal, and free moment they had together. Their lust for one another was insatiable. They were intimate as often as possible; wherever they could find a little privacy. It was both naughty and exhilarating. When they could keep their hands off each other, they traveled. Together Lauren and Davin wandered the streets and toured the sights of Baltimore, Philadelphia, Washington D.C., and New York. As their graduation date drew near, Lauren hoped Davin would be stationed closer to her even though he had his heart set on Rota, Spain. Lauren knew she would deploy sometime after she returned home to her Army Reserve Detachment, but selfishly she wanted him with her as long as possible.

One day, Davin excitedly met Lauren for dinner at the chow hall. "I have news. I'm going to Rota. My next assignment will be at the Naval Media Center there," he said.

Lauren feigned excitement, "That's wonderful. I'm glad you got what you wanted." Davin knew Lauren, and he knew when something was wrong. "Lauren, it's going to be okay. We will make it through this." Lauren believed him. She replied, "I hope so."

Graduation day came with the usual pomp and circumstance. As Lauren dressed in her Army dress uniform, she was both proud of her accomplishments and somber. The day would be bittersweet. The Army had given her orders and arranged to send her home to Texas to report to her detachment the following day. The Navy had not yet issued Davin's orders. He would have to stay at Fort Meade while his paperwork was processed. Lauren scolded herself as she stood in front of the mirror in her room thinking about Davin and straightening her uniform. *"You shouldn't have done this to yourself,"* she said. Lauren snatched her beret off her bed, left her room, and headed down the stairs to meet the other graduating Army students. They all left the barracks together and headed to the schoolhouse to have their class photo taken before the ceremony. She could see Davin ahead of them with his group. She could always tell which sailor he was in a crowd from his gait. She smiled as she watched him walk. She was the happiest she'd ever been since meeting Davin. She loved him so much.

As the groups converged, Davin approached her. "Hey, are you going to have some time later?"

Lauren still needed to pack her things for her departure the next morning. "Probably not. I haven't wanted to pack anything. I've been procrastinating because packing means I'll have to say goodbye to you, too. I haven't wanted to think about any of it," she said. Lauren wished Davin could hug and kiss her. She wanted him to reassure her, but he couldn't. They were in uniform, and their relationship was still a secret because of the rules. Just then, the photographer arrived. He asked them to situate themselves. Lauren stood in the front row at parade rest with her hands placed in the small of her back. Davin positioned himself behind her. While the graduates and instructors were posed and distracted by the photographer, Davin utilized the opportunity to press the front of his hand against Lauren's palm. His gesture was a comforting and welcome one. At that moment, Lauren knew no matter where the military took them or how long they were separated this man truly loved her, and her heart would be eternally lost without him. He was the love of her life. He was her soul mate.

After the graduation, Lauren rushed back to the barracks to change her uniform and pack her things. She also needed to launder and return her issued linen to barracks supply. In the morning, she'd have a final room inspection. Lauren needed to make sure everything was clean and in order. She gave away all the personal items she could and folded the rest into her Army duffle bags. The task took her most of the evening to complete. When she finished, Lauren contemplated how she would manage to get it all to the airport. Seven months of her life sat in front of her packed neatly into four drab green bags. There were only four. They were heavy, but it could have been worse.

She called Davin, and he answered, "Hi, sweetheart. Are you alright?"

She replied, "Yes and no. I don't know. I just need a ride to the airport in the morning if you're available. If not I can call a taxi."

Davin responded, "You'd better not call a cab. Of course, I'll take you. I've been worried about you. What time would you like me to pick you up?"

Lauren and Davin agreed on a time. She was glad to have his help and support. Before hanging up, she apologized, "I'm sorry. I'm just not good at feelings or goodbyes. I never expected to find you."

In an attempt to lighten her seriousness she said, "I love you Shnuga Booga."

Davin responded, "I love you too. I'll be there for you tomorrow, and every other day you'll have me."

The next morning Lauren signed out of the Army barracks and hauled her bags to the curb to wait on Davin. He pulled up just as she was setting the last one down.

He popped his trunk and hopped out of the car. "Did you carry these by yourself?" he asked.

She smiled and confidently announced, "I'm an American soldier." They both loaded her things into his car and set off for the airport. Lauren was disheartened. She did not want to leave Davin. Davin knew this and could not bear to see her so sad. He loved her smile and hated when it was missing. Davin knew she desperately needed a reprieve from her gloom and was determined to prove today would not be the end of their relationship.

On the way to the airport, Davin mentioned, "I'm going to be here for a couple of weeks with nothing to do. Do you think after you check in with your unit you'd like to come back and keep me company? I'll pay for everything." Lauren felt instantly cured of her blues.

Lauren kissed his cheek and laid her head on his shoulder. "I would love to keep you company. I just want to be with you," she said. Davin rested his head against hers and continued to drive.

When they arrived at the airport, Lauren checked her bags and got her ticket. She mentally tried to prepare herself.

She began, "I love you so much, Davin. I..." Davin placed all the tips of his fingers on her lips and shushed her. Lauren thought he was hilarious. They stayed standing that way until she stopped laughing.

Then he said, "We're not saying goodbye. You told me you were coming back, remember? I'm going to kiss you, but only because I enjoy doing it so much. When you land, call me. I need to know you made it home safely." Lauren stood silently absorbing his words. She was an emotional mess who was barely keeping it together.

He always knew what to say. "Lauren, listen to me and believe me when I say, everything will be okay. Once you've checked in with your detachment, let me know, and I'll put you on the next plane back. I will always love you and take care of you. I'm your Shnuga Booga."

Lauren laughed with tears in her eyes. She kissed him with all the passion she thought was acceptable for a public place. Afterward, he walked with her over to the line to pass through security. Lauren cleared the screening and looked back one last time. Davin was still there. They waved at each other and parted ways.

Lauren landed in San Antonio, Texas. Her unit was located at Fort Sam Houston. She lived in New Braunfels, so it was a convenient commute to her monthly Battle Assembly. She missed Davin immensely but was ecstatic to see the Lone Star State. She'd also missed her sister, Judy, who lived with her. Lauren had three siblings. She and Judy had always been closest. Lauren shared a six-year age difference with her littlest sister, Ariel and a ten-year difference with her brother, Aiden, but she and Judy were only one year apart. Riding down the escalator to baggage claim, she scanned the crowd until she spotted her waving. They were happy to see each other.

When she reached the bottom, Lauren made her way over to her and hugged her. "Thank you for picking me up! I'm so glad you're here because I need help carrying my bags."

Judy laughed and said, "Thanks."

They waited for Lauren's bags and updated each other on the changes in their lives from the last seven months. They had only been able to speak to each other a few times while Lauren was away and those conversations had been brief.

Judy announced, "I have a new boyfriend. His name is Cliff. Oh, and my college classes are going great."

Lauren replied, "That's good. Is Cliff nice?" Lauren listened as Judy told her all about her new man. She could relate to her enthusiasm. When Lauren's bags arrived, they each grabbed two off the conveyer belt. Then they exited the airport and found Judy's car.

Once settled inside the vehicle Lauren shared, "I've missed you so much, and I appreciate you picking me up, but you'll have to drop me off again soon. I'm going back to Maryland."

Judy questioned, "Why? I thought you were done?"

Lauren continued, "I am, but I also have a new boyfriend." As the word came out of her mouth, Lauren realized it was the first time she'd called Davin her boyfriend. She also noted she could say it aloud to whomever she pleased. The rules did not apply anymore. Lauren and Judy chatted about their newfound loves the entire way home. Lauren could not wait to see her house, sleep in her bed, and enjoy her things. She was also eager to call Davin to let him know she made it safely.

Judy pulled into the garage and parked.

In excitement, Lauren exclaimed, "My car!" She was so happy to be home. They unloaded Lauren's bags and pilled them against the wall in her bedroom. Lauren was tired from a long day of airports, flight delays, and feelings. She was ready to crawl into her very own bed for the first time in forever.

Lauren found Judy in her room. "Hey, I'm turning in early if that's okay with you? I'd like to call Davin. I also need to go to my detachment tomorrow," she said.

Judy consented, "Yeah, that's fine. I'll probably meet my boyfriend later anyway." Lauren headed to her room and closed the door. She wandered around naked enjoying the freedom of her space. She could have taken all the time in the world to bathe if she wanted, but instead hopped in and out of the shower. She wrapped her towel around her and grabbed her phone from the nightstand to call Davin.

He answered, "Hey, baby."

She responded, "I miss you, boyfriend. I realized I can say that now."

Davin laughed and replied, "I miss you too. Did you get there okay?" Lauren told him all about her airport adventure and conversation with Judy.

Davin listened attentively. "I'm glad you made it home safely," he said.

Lauren went on, "I'm going to my unit in the morning. I'll let you know when I can come back." As they hung up, they wished each other sweet dreams. Lauren drifted to sleep with the knowledge she would see Davin soon and the acceptance that telephoned hellos and goodbyes would be a recurring event in their long-distance relationship. They would have to remain committed to their bond and dedicated to stealing every available opportunity to be together. Lauren felt confident in their love for each other and knew they were capable of anything.

The next morning Lauren put on her uniform and drove to Fort Sam Houston to report as ordered. She met the MPAD's administrator, Sergeant First Class Camp, for the first time.

He greeted her, "Hello, Private Mayer. How was it?"

Lauren replied, "I had a great time. I learned a lot, Sergeant."

"That's great. I hope you're ready for your first assignment. There's a retirement ceremony we're sending you to in Dallas," he said. Lauren realized she would not be able to see Davin as soon as she had hoped.

He continued, "We received a request from the Broadcast Operations Detachment this falls under. They are unable to send a broadcaster because they're currently preparing to deploy. I need you to film it. I'll send the footage to them for editing. I'm working on your orders today."

He pointed to the current date on his desk calendar. It was a Friday. He then moved his finger across to the following Monday. "Be ready to go Monday morning."

Lauren replied, "Yes, Sergeant." She listened as he explained his expectations. He handed her a tentative schedule for the event.

He then informed her, "It will be a quick trip. You'll be gone twenty-four hours tops. The next weekend you'll meet the rest of the unit at Battle Assembly. It's December, so we'll have a dress uniform inspection. Also, for our two-week training event, we're going to Japan. Our detachment will provide the public affairs support for Operation North Wind. It's a yearly field training exercise between Japan's army and ours. That'll be in February. Then there's the deployment. Right now it looks like Afghanistan."

Lauren absorbed it all nodding her head in acknowledgment and confirming, "Got it, Sergeant." The Sergeant issued her a camera and the necessary accessories to complete her mission. She thanked him and left the office. As Lauren drove away from the base, she was still reeling from all the information she'd gotten. Lauren knew Davin would be just as disappointed as she was when she told him she could not join him back at Fort Meade anytime soon. Christmas was coming, and they'd both have family obligations. If she were going to see Davin stateside, it would have to be after the holidays and before his departure to Spain and hers to Japan.

That evening, Lauren called Davin to break the news. She counted the telephone rings hoping he would answer.

When he did, she told him, "I have bad news." Lauren repeated the information she'd received earlier. She was extremely discouraged and questioned, "Davin, is this going to work or are we just kidding ourselves? Was Ms. Tanya right?"

Davin calmly said, "Stop it, Lauren. I know what we'll do. I'll request leave from the Navy barracks and come to you. I don't have anything to do here except wait. I haven't been to Texas in a while. I'd like to see you. See your home. Meet your sister."

"You'd do that," Lauren asked.

Davin went on, "I will tell you as often as you need me to. I would do anything for you. I'll just time it so when you're coming back from Dallas I'll be arriving too. Then we can both leave the airport together."

"I don't know any of my ticket information until check-in," she told him.

"That's fine. You tell me when you know and I'll be there," he assured. Lauren already knew this man was her perfect match, but he proved it further every day. Her weaknesses were his strengths. He was the answer to every question and the comfort to every doubt. Davin and Lauren said their usual goodnights. She hung up the phone, opened her door, and left her room to find Judy. She needed to tell her what she'd be doing the next couple of days. Judy was not difficult to find. The smell of burnt food and sight of smoke filling the house gave away her location immediately.

Lauren ran to the kitchen, "What on earth are you doing?"

The smoke alarm began to chime. Judy was panicked, "I don't know!" Lauren told her to take care of the alarm while she turned off the stove. Then she grabbed an oven mitt and hauled the hot pan out into the backyard.

On her way out the door she yelled, "Are you trying to burn down the house?" After the situation was resolved, Judy came outside where Lauren was checking the pan to see if it had cooled sufficiently.

She said, "I wanted to make you dinner tonight. I invited my boyfriend, Cliff, over to meet you. I just wanted to do something nice." Lauren had always prepared the meals when she was home. She was an excellent cook, but it had been awhile since she'd dominated her kitchen. Lauren thought about it and decided it was time to reacquaint herself.

After all, Davin was coming to spend time with her, and he would need to eat. "I tell you what; we will start over. I'll make dinner and you can…"

Lauren searched her mind for something to give Judy to do. "You can air out the house and light some candles? If your boyfriend asks, we'll tell him you cooked the meal."

Lauren smiled at her, "Come on. Tell me what was on the menu."

Judy laughed and gave her the rundown. Then they both headed back into the house to complete their tasks before Judy's company arrived.

Lauren awoke with a start and looked at her bedside alarm clock. It was zero seven hundred hours. Lauren could not believe she'd slept in so late. Lauren heard the front door close. She got out of bed and ran to catch Judy just as she was leaving with Cliff. They had all been up late the night before talking, and Cliff had stayed over. He was taking Judy on a trip, but before they left Lauren needed to talk to her.

She opened the front door and hollered, "Judy!" Judy rolled down the passenger window.

Lauren walked over and continued, "I don't need you to take me to the airport anymore. I'm not going back to Maryland. I have to do this assignment for my detachment on Monday. I am going somewhere, but I'll just park my car at the airport since I'll be back the next day. Also, my boyfriend, Davin is coming to visit."

"Okay," said Judy.

She continued, "I talked to mom this morning. I was going to call you later when you were awake. Ariel and Aiden are on Christmas break and want to visit. I'm going to pick them up Tuesday."

Judy leaned out her window with arms outstretched. "I'm glad you're home. Call me if you need anything." Lauren hugged her, told her she would, and backed away so they could pull out of the driveway. She waved as she watched them go realizing she was alone. Lauren returned inside and locked the door behind her. She had no idea what she was going to do to pass the time. She had not been alone in what felt like an eternity. Lauren decided to unpack her bags. While doing so, she came across the hundreds of pictures she and Davin had taken from their time together. She would have loved to call him and reminisce on the phone all weekend, but the notion was an impractical one. Instead, she dug out her scrapbooking supplies. Lauren loved scrapbooking. The hobby was one she picked up in high school after joining the yearbook staff. She enjoyed playing with layouts and designs. Lauren decided scrapbooking her life with Davin, was the perfect distraction. Her weekend flew by with ease. When she spoke with Davin she told him all about her project. He seemed more interested in flight details. Lauren promised to call him as soon as she checked in at the airport the next morning. It had only been a few days, but they could not wait to be together again.

Lauren awoke early and dressed in her uniform. She called her Sergeant to confirm her departure time. He informed her the flight would leave at eleven hundred hours. Lauren had just enough time to drive from New Braunfels to the San Antonio International Airport. She quickly grabbed the overnight bag she'd packed the night before and her camera. When she arrived, she parked her car and checked in. Her orders were waiting just as her Sergeant said they would be. Lauren was relieved everything was going smoothly. She inquired about her flight itinerary and was handed a printout by the man assisting her. After passing through security and finding her gate, she called Davin as promised.

He answered, "I'm so glad you called."

Lauren laughed, "We hardly ever say hello to each other. We just start our conversations as if we're in the middle of them. I love that about us."

Davin laughed, "Me too. Anyway, when can I fly to you?" He was eager to buy his ticket.

Lauren said, "According to this itinerary I'll be returning tomorrow at ten hundred. Don't forget you're one hour ahead."

Davin responded, "Noted, my love."

Lauren heard the call to board. "We're boarding. I need to go."

Davin empathized, "I've got stuff to do, too. If I don't talk to you, know I'm thinking about you and wish you lots of luck at your thing. See you tomorrow!"

Lauren responded, "I love you." She stood and boarded her flight. Everything was going as planned. When she arrived, a fellow soldier picked her up from the airport and escorted her to the location where the ceremony was taking place. She had plenty of time to set up her equipment and film the ceremony. Afterward, the same comrade took her to a hotel for the night. She called Davin to ask about his flight information. He told her he'd be arriving a little before her at zero nine thirty. The next morning Lauren took a shuttle from the hotel back to the airport for her flight to San Antonio. On the plane, she contemplated how much her life had changed. She'd never flown anywhere until she joined the military. Now between the Army and Davin, she would be on airplanes all the time.

Lauren touched down in San Antonio and found Davin at baggage claim.

She hugged him and whispered in his ear, "Let's get out of here so I can make love to you."

Davin kissed her hard. "Let's go," he said.

They gathered their bags as quickly as possible and made the drive to her house. When they arrived, Lauren noted Judy's car was gone. Judy did tell her she would be picking up their little brother and sister. Lauren mentioned this to Davin as they exited her vehicle. They did not even bother unloading their bags. Instead, they headed straight for her bedroom where she removed his clothing and pushed him back onto the bed. She undressed and climbed on top of him. Lauren teased him by grabbing his shaft and inserting his tip into her a few times before slowly sliding onto him. She felt whole when his perfectly erect penis was inside her. Lauren began to rock her hips against his. Davin sat up slightly to reach her perky breasts. From their previous encounters, he knew she would cum quickly if he played with them. He caressed her hard nipples with his tongue as she continued to thrust against his tight embrace until she came.

Afterward, she stopped, and breathlessly teased again, "I'm done. That was so good for me. Thank you."

As she dismounted with a smile, Davin grabbed her arm, "I don't think so, my love. Get back here."

Davin stood and positioned her to bend over the bed. Lauren complied. While reaching for pillows to make herself more comfortable, he firmly grabbed her hips and entered her from behind. He felt incredible. They were puzzle pieces fashioned to fit together flawlessly. Lauren closed her eyes and panted in pleasure. Davin continued to drive himself into her until he came. Again, she felt the familiar throbbing of his release. When he finished, he leaned forward and kissed her back. They both fell into bed, naked, and intertwined. Lauren, who had recently been immersed in scrapbooking, reached over and opened the drawer of her nightstand to pull out her camera.

She snapped a picture of them and said, "We can't take a naked nap now."

Davin was disappointed and asked, "Why not?" Lauren explained, "My siblings are coming and I wanted to hang lights and put up the Christmas tree before they got here. Ariel is fourteen and Aiden is ten. It's the kind of thing they'd love. I have boxes full of Christmas stuff in the garage."

Davin agreed to help her with a kiss and a condition. "I'll put the lights on the house, and you can decorate anything else you want, but first, we take a shower. Deal?" Lauren agreed and got out of bed to turn on the water. They both got in and took turns lathering each other up, enjoying each other's touch, and embracing in the cascade falling over them.

Judy arrived later that evening with Ariel and Aiden to a beautifully lit and decoratively transformed home. Lauren and Davin had spent the afternoon creating a Christmas ambiance for them all. Lauren introduced them to Davin. Later, they left for an evening on the San Antonio River Walk. The walk, covered in lights, was stunning. Lauren took lots of pictures, and Davin treated them to dinner. It was a perfect evening. Her brother and sisters seemed to like him very much. When they returned home, Ariel and Aiden confirmed their approval as Lauren told them goodnight. Lauren was also impressed with Davin. She had never seen him around children. He had entertained and played with them seamlessly. Lauren checked on Judy who was in her room.

She informed her, "The little ones are down. They should be out soon. I locked the doors and shut down the house."

Judy replied, "Thanks."

As Lauren turned to leave, Judy stopped her, "Hey, Lauren. He seems nice. I'm glad you're happy."

Lauren said, "Me too." Lauren was happy.

She returned to her room to find Davin who had already made himself comfortable in her bed. She changed into a silky nightgown and climbed in next to him. Lauren put her head on his chest pressing her ear against it to listen to his heartbeat.

"The verdict is in. They said they like you," she reported.

He replied, "Good. I like them too."

Lauren adored the timbre of his voice. She asked, "Do you want children someday?"

Davin said, "Yes. I want our children. I can imagine waking up late on the weekend with a little you and a little me running around our room or jumping on our bed with us still in it. I think about how mischievous a little Lauren would be or how calm and sweet a little Davin would be."

Lauren laughed, "Why does our daughter have to be mischievous?" Lauren knew why he envisioned her this way. She had once shared a story about sitting in church debating if the spanking her mother had promised beforehand was worth climbing under the pews. Unfortunately for her mother, the pastor, and the congregation she rarely missed an opportunity to low crawl her way to the front even though she knew the repercussions. Davin loved this story.

He smiled and said, "Because she'd be everything you are and she'd be perfect." Lauren and Davin continued to discuss the possible qualities of their future children and exchanged stories from their childhoods until they both fell asleep dreaming of the family that could be.

Eventually, the week ended and everyone departed. Judy left to return Ariel and Aiden. Davin headed back to Fort Meade, and Lauren reported to her unit's Battle Assembly. On the last day they spent together, Lauren and Davin sat down with her calendar and made a plan. Lauren's month included her military duties and a trip to Saltillo, Mexico with her family to visit their relatives. Davin would be going to North Carolina to be with his family. In January, they agreed to meet back at Fort Meade. February included international trips for them both. Lauren's orders were to Camp Higashi-Chitose in Hokkaido, Japan and Davin's orders were to Rota, Spain. They agreed Davin would need a few weeks to adjust to his new duty station and find a place to live. After her March Battle Assembly, Lauren would fly to Spain to spend time with Davin. She'd return in time to report for April's reserve duty. She wasn't sure when her detachment would begin preparations for deployment to Afghanistan, but she was sure nothing would happen before May.

Lauren was examining their notations on her calendar and said, "We're not going to be able to talk as often with all this maneuvering."

Davin chimed in with another of his ideas, "We could write letters during the times we can't talk. Then we could still connect with each other just on a delay. We'd be like the service members of old."

Lauren liked this idea, "We're journalist, right? No one writes letters anymore. I love it. It's romantic."

Lauren and Davin promised to write and call each other as often as possible. Before he left, Lauren slipped a Christmas gift into his suitcase. She'd finished the scrapbook and wanted him to have it. Lauren thought it might be tough for Davin to be in a new place without her. She hoped the photos would remind him of the fun times they'd shared and their love for one another. Along with it, she included their first letter.

Davin,

Your tender spirit and boyish charm make you the most precious and unforgettable person I've ever known. I thank God every day for putting you in my life. You are my soul mate. Being with you makes so much sense. Distance and time can never keep us apart. I've found you. I know I can't be with you, but I'll do what I have to do to keep our love alive. I won't ever let you go, my love. I need you too much. Understand that our time apart from one another may be difficult, but it's worth the happiness we'll find together in the end. I dream about our life and the beautiful family we'll make. I promise one day I'll return all the happiness and love you've given me. I love you so much, Shnuga Booga. My heart has found great comfort in you. Thank you for always understanding and being the kind, caring person you are. Thank you for not giving up on me even when I'm difficult.

Davin, I've never wanted anything so badly in my life. I yearn for a time when we can wake up next to each other every morning. I wish you were here with me now. I miss you so much. Remember, I'm waiting here patiently for you, my love. Cherish my heart and keep it safe. I'll do the same with yours.

Hugs and Kisses,
Your Lauren.

P.S. I've left the last pages in this scrapbook blank. I want to fill them with our adventures from Spain.

Chapter 5

Lauren was on her way to Seville, Spain. Her passport had become her most prized possession. She was on her second international trip within the first few months of the New Year. She slept most of the flight to avoid any jet lag she might have upon landing. She was eager to see Davin. He had written her about his adventures. He promised to save some of the sights on his list for them to explore together. Truthfully, Lauren didn't care if they never left his bedroom, but Davin was a wanderer, and she loved him enough to follow him wherever his heart desired. Lauren's flight landed, and she disembarked to make her way to baggage claim. She spotted Davin immediately. They walked briskly toward each other. She noticed his beautiful blonde hair, which she loved to run her fingers through when they were making love, was not visible beneath the baseball cap he was wearing.

She asked, "Did you shave your head?"

Davin answered, "Yeah. It was thinning and making me self-conscious, so I shaved it. I save a lot on haircuts now."

Lauren kissed him. "I don't care. You always look yummy to me," she said.

Davin hugged her tightly picking her up off the ground. "I've missed you," he replied.

She kissed him again and responded, "I've missed you too, Shnuga."

Airport reunions had become a regular occurrence. They'd also developed a custom of snatching bags from baggage claim and making a beeline for seclusion to reacquaint themselves. This day was no different. Davin drove her to his home in Costa Ballena as quickly as possible. His apartment was on the second story in a vacation complex. It had a large, semi-walled terrace overlooking the ocean and an adjoining park.

There was also a golf course next door. Davin explained, "It's off-season right now. Nobody lives here except me. We have the place all to ourselves." Lauren loved the ocean, and here it would be just theirs. She knew they were both ready to commence some well-deserved lovemaking, but after seeing the water, she desperately wanted to explore the beach. As she stood in the brisk wind whipping up from the waves, she took in the beauty of the sunset and listened to the subtle song of the tide.

Davin watched her intently. "Isn't it beautiful?"

Lauren replied, "Yes. Can we go? I want to put my toes in the sand."

"Right now," he asked. "I've been traveling forever."

She pleaded, "Please?" Davin could not say no, and agreed. Lauren quickly changed into her bathing suit and grabbed a shawl before they made the short walk down to the water. As they strolled through the lapping of the shallow waves holding hands and talking about how much they'd missed each other, Lauren became incredibly aroused. She'd once seen a movie where the actors romped on the beach. She had always thought sex on the beach was a terrible idea and completely impractical due to the stickiness of the sand and a body's nooks and crannies. However, she did have her shawl, and they were alone. Lauren could not help herself. She stopped, laid it out on the ground, and sat down on it. Davin sat down next to her.

They watched the waves for a moment before Lauren turned to him and asked, "If I wanted to make love to you right here, right now would you let me?"

Davin must have been thinking the same thing. With lust in his eyes, he nodded his head silently consenting. Lauren leaned in, and they began to kiss passionately. Davin ran his hand up under her bikini top to caress her breast while Lauren unzipped his shorts. She saw he was erect.

Lauren kissed his neck and whispered, "Do me from behind."

They each positioned themselves on their knees facing the ocean. Lauren leaned forward to support herself. With one arm planted, she reached between her legs with the other and pulled the crotch of her bikini to one side. Davin entered her forcefully as if he desperately needed her warmth. The intensity consumed her as he thrust harder and harder. Lauren became increasingly wet from the friction. He continued to hold one hip with his hand. He reached around with the other to play with her. His coaxing overtook her. She liked to let him know when she was about to climax so they could do so together. She called out to him through her groans of desire. As they both began to succumb to the pleasure, he grabbed her hips with both hands and pulled her into him as if he could not

47

be deep enough for his impending explosion. She felt his release inside her. Lauren was pleased she turned him on as much as he did her.

While recovering, Lauren sat between Davin's outstretched legs and leaned back against him. Davin wrapped his arms around her and rested his chin against her shoulder. Periodically he would kiss her neck.

She loved how naughty she felt. "Are you satisfied, man of mine?" she asked.

He assured her, "Very."

They stayed on the beach watching the sun as it finished setting into the horizon.

When the last rays of light disappeared into the ocean, Davin said, "Come on, lover. Let's get something to eat." Lauren and Davin found a sandwich shop and ordered.

As they sat eating their bocadillos and drinking tinto, Davin informed her, "Don't get too used to this. Tomorrow, I'm taking you to the grocery store. I miss your delicious food. I want you to cook me some home cooked meals."

Lauren jested, "Come on? I'm on vacation. I didn't know the commissary was on our sightseeing list."

She secretly loved that Davin appreciated her skills in the kitchen. When he had visited her, he complimented and had seconds every meal.

Davin begged, "Please? You know you could cook a shoelace and make it taste good."

Lauren yielded, "Alright. I'll make you whatever you want, but you will take me out for dinner occasionally."

"As you wish," he said. They devoured their meals and returned to Davin's apartment for the night. Lauren was exhausted, and Davin had work in the morning. She wished he could stay to entertain her, but he was new to the Naval Media Center and the host of a four-hour, weekday radio show. Lauren understood. She would just have to entertain herself while he was working.

The next morning Lauren awoke to the sounds of Davin preparing to leave for work.

She left the bedroom to find him. "Good morning, Shnuga Booga," she said.

He was shaving and could see her behind him in the mirror. "I'm sorry, sweetheart. I didn't mean to wake you. You looked peaceful."

Lauren asked, "Were you going to leave without saying goodbye?" She made her way to the toilet and sat down. Lauren had an overactive bladder. She'd learned long ago, when she needed to go she should. This inhibition was further reinforced during basic training where facilities weren't always available. Lauren knew how to pee without shame, and she desperately needed to release the contents of her bladder.

Davin stopped and looked over at her. "We've never done this before. Should I leave?"

Lauren laughed loudly. "I guess we haven't. This isn't more intimate than sex, and we've done that more times than I can count. I know you get the milk for free, but if you ever decide to buy the cow, this will probably happen again."

Davin continued to shave looking puzzled. "Did you just call yourself a cow?" he asked.

Lauren flushed, and made her way over to the sink to wash her hands. "It's a saying," she retorted. "Why buy the cow when you can get the milk for free."

Davin finished shaving and sat his razor down. He smiled, kissed, and wiped his cheek on hers transferring the remaining shaving cream to her face. Lauren sighed heavily in annoyance.

Davin laughed and remarked, "Oh, no! My cow is mad." He picked up a washcloth that was lying on the edge sink and wiped the foam from both their faces.

Davin squeezed her tight and assured her in a Texas twang, "Trust me. I'm gonna buy this peeing cow someday. She's fancy!" Lauren giggled. She liked the thought of being Mrs. Lauren Hendrix. She followed him as he exited the bathroom and gathered his things to head out the door. She did feel like his wife kissing him goodbye as he went off to work.

Before Davin left, he instructed, "Turn on the radio in the living room at ten. I already programmed it to our station. I'll pick you up after work to go to the commissary."

He kissed her goodbye. "I love you, Bessie."

Lauren kissed him back. As he headed down the stairs, she hollered, "Don't ever call me that again!"

Lauren shut the door, locked it, and made her way to the terrace. The sun was just beginning to rise. The smell of the ocean was intoxicating. Lauren wanted to call Judy to let her know she had arrived safely, but the time difference was seven hours, and she'd be asleep. Lauren was still incredibly tired, and she decided to go back to bed. She drifted off quickly to the sounds of the waves lulling her to sleep. Later, Lauren awoke with a start. Davin's home phone was ringing in the hallway. She looked at the bedside clock before running to answer it.

It was almost twelve, "Hello?"

Davin answered, "It's me. Who'd you think it would be?"

Lauren responded, "The phone woke me up. I fell asleep after you left."

Davin continued, "Dang. You missed the beginning of the show. I told the listeners about my soldier."

"I'm sorry," she said. "I slept most of the flight, but I have jet lag anyway."

Davin went on, "It's okay. Wait? Are you sure it's the jet lag? You're not upset with me for calling you Bessie, are you?"

Lauren knew he was teasing and teased back, "I should be. I should also be furious you're taking me grocery shopping on base instead of site seeing this evening!"

Lauren turned on the radio. "Okay, I've got you on now. I'm awake and listening."

"Muah," he said. "I've got to go."

"Muah," she replied. Lauren grabbed the radio and hauled it out to the terrace. The sun was high in the sky, and she was alone. Lauren decided it was the perfect opportunity for naked sunbathing. She retrieved a towel and spread it out. After disrobing, she laid down to soak in the Spanish rays. Lauren listened to the music and realized the format of Davin's show was classic rock. She thought it was fitting since he adored this genre of music. The song ended, and Davin began to speak, "Hey! You're listening to Devastatin' Davin."

Lauren laughed. Of course, he had a cheesy handle too. "I just got off the phone with my girl. You guys were right. She has an excellent sense of humor, but calling her Bessie this morning may not have been my smoothest move. Also, telling her I was taking her to the commissary for her first outing in Spain didn't win me any brownie points. Give me a call if you have a request. Keep the nicknames coming. I need a new one for her. A good one, or tonight I'm getting the cold shoulder for sure. This one goes out to you, Lauren. Here's the Rolling Stones with 'She's So Cold'."

The song began to play. Lauren assumed Davin had used their morning conversation for show material. She smirked as she listened. Davin often pulled this song from his repertoire to redirect her when she was irritated with him. His impersonation of Mick

Jagger, complete with dance moves, usually did the trick. Lauren searched her mind a moment and called the station.

Davin answered, "This is Devastatin' Davin. What can I do for you?"

Lauren flirted, "Yes. I'm sunbathing naked on my boyfriend's terrace."

Davin recognized her voice. "Oh, really?"

"Uh-huh. Anyway, I heard you talking about your lame girlfriend, and I have a proposal. She seems like high maintenance and my boyfriend is always at work. What do you say we ditch them?"

Davin joked, "Miss, I am flattered, but I couldn't possibly. I've already put a lot of work into fixing her."

"Fine then, I'd like to request a song," she said. "It's not a classic."

Davin laughed, "Okay. What do you want to hear?" Lauren made her request and hung up.

When the song that was playing ended, Davin came back on. "Up next is Sheryl Crow, 'Soak up the Sun'. This one goes out to a naked, sunbathing beauty on some lucky sailor's terrace."

After Davin's show ended, Lauren called Judy to let her know she was okay. She then made her way to the bathroom to draw a bath. It was located at the end of a long hallway connected to the living room. She filled the claw foot tub, climbed in, and sank into the coolness of the water. It felt refreshing. Lauren wished Davin were home. It would be a few more hours before she saw him. While soaking, Lauren hummed a song she'd heard on the radio. After singing some of the lyrics, she realized the bathroom had great acoustics. Lauren was singing her heart out and tapping her foot against the porcelain when she heard the front door open and close. From the tub, she could see straight into the living room. Lauren lowered her voice and watched the hall. She was preparing to exit the bath when Davin finally stepped into view.

She yelled, "You scared me!"

Davin walked toward the bathroom. "I'm sorry. I didn't mean to scare you. I wanted to surprise you. My Chief let me leave work early. I could hear you singing downstairs, and I didn't want to interrupt. I didn't know you could sing."

"Of course, you scared me. You're not supposed to be home until later," she said.

Davin, looking at her the way he did when he was mesmerized, said, "Lauren, you really are perfect. I don't think there's anything you can't do."

Lauren stood up and stepped out of the tub. "You know, admitting you have a problem is the first step," she said.

Davin questioned, "Problem?"

Lauren grabbed a towel and wrapped it around her. "Yeah, it's the first step to overcoming your Lauren addiction."

Davin picked her up and threw her over his shoulder. "What are you doing," she asked.

Davin carried her to his bedroom where he tossed her on the bed. "I'll admit I'm a Lauren addict, but I have no intention of ever overcoming it."

Davin grabbed Lauren's towel and unwrapped it before roughly pulling it out from under her. Then he undressed. Lauren's sailor had manhandled her, and it turned her on.

She feigned ignorance. "What's happening right now?"

Davin crawled on top of her and said, "I need a fix." Lauren bit her lip in delight as he entered her. Aroused by his aggression, she let him have his way.

Lauren and Davin eventually made it to the commissary on base. They discussed dinner ideas and Davin selected some of his favorites. While wandering the aisles of the grocery store collecting ingredients Davin mentioned, "I talked to my Chief about you. He wants to meet you. He said I could leave after my show while you're here."

Lauren remarked, "Wow! That's generous."

Davin continued, "We can do our local sightseeing in the afternoons and evenings and the farther stuff this weekend." Lauren would only be there a short time and wanted to see as much as possible.

"That sounds perfect," she said.

Davin asked, "Do you want to come to the station tomorrow? The Chief said it was okay. I told him you're a broadcaster too." Lauren didn't want to feel uncomfortable.

She replied, "I don't know. What would I do? You have physical training and other duties before your show even starts. I don't want to be the awkward Army tourist of the Naval Media Center."

"Alright," said Davin.

"How about I pick you up right before my show starts and introduce you to everyone. Then you can sit in the radio booth with me?" Lauren liked this idea much better.

She agreed, "I can do that." Davin paid for their items, and they left to head home. When they arrived, they each grabbed a few bags and climbed the stairs. Lauren was unloading the groceries when she noticed a box on the dining room table.

She asked Davin, "That box wasn't here earlier, was it?"

Davin smiled and went to retrieve it. "I was going to give it to you before, but I got distracted."

He handed it to Lauren, and she opened it. Inside was a beautiful teal ribbon knit sweater.

"Davin, it's stunning," she said. He kissed her on the cheek as she examined it.

"I saw it when I was walking to a bar to meet the guys the other day." He continued, "I knew you'd like it, so I stopped and bought it for you. I had it at the office to send to you, but I decided to wait until you got here instead." Lauren thanked him and put it away. Her thoughtful man deserved a thoughtful meal. After dinner, they sat on the terrace sipping wine and enjoying each other's company.

The next day Lauren awoke to Davin leaving for work. He gave her a key so she could come and go as she pleased. Davin reminded Lauren he would pick her up later. She kissed him goodbye, and he left. Lauren decided to kill time with a run. She'd noticed a beachfront boardwalk on their first visit to the shoreline. Lauren stretched and set out to exercise. It was a beautiful morning. She ran to the end of the walk and turned around. Lauren was thoroughly enjoying her workout when she spotted something ahead. It appeared to be two dogs planted in the middle of the pathway. They had not been there before when she passed. As she approached, they did not seem like they were going to move. Lauren slowed to a walk. She wasn't sure if they were friendly or not. Lauren was almost even with them when she realized they were strays. Both seemed approachable, so she put her hand out to the one closest to her. She was female and appeared to be pregnant. Her male companion was protective, but not aggressive. After sniffing her out, they both decided she was okay.

Lauren could tell they were hungry. She looked over the two as she pet them. Through their dull coats, she noticed their bones were visible from malnutrition. Lauren checked her watch. If she cut her workout short, she'd have enough time to retrieve some food, deliver it, and get back to shower before Davin arrived to pick her up. Lauren left the walk and headed for the apartment. She looked back to note the location so she could find them again, but realized they were following her. Lauren was glad. If they followed her back, she could save some time. Lauren arrived at the gate to Davin's apartment complex. She left both dogs sitting there and ran up the stairs to grab some leftovers. When she returned, she talked to them as she divided the remnants of last night's meal.

"I hope you like it as much as Davin did," she said.

"This was supposed to be my lunch." They scarfed it down and wagged their tales in appreciation. The female was black and tan with white toes, and the male was white and brown with white on the tapered end of his tail.

Lauren continued to pet and talk to them as if they understood her. "I'll come find you later, momma. You take care of her, daddy. I've got to go, okay?"

They seemed like they were pleased. Lauren told them goodbye and ran back up the stairs to the apartment to get ready. She showered quickly and dressed in a black and white striped tank top and white pencil skirt. Lauren was in the bedroom finishing her hair and makeup when Davin opened the front door.

He hollered from the living room, "Lauren, are you ready?"

Lauren grabbed her high heels from her suitcase. "Yes. I'm coming." She headed down the hallway stopping mid-stride to put each shoe on. When she reached him, she stood up straight and adjusted her skirt.

He examined her and remarked, "You are going to cause problems at the Media Center dressed like that. Why are you always so sexy?"

Lauren retorted, "I'm sexy because God made me this way and you like it!" Davin kissed her as if he was ready to undress her. Lauren broke away from his lips and said,

"We can do sexy stuff later, Shnuga Booga." She hated being late and knew Davin needed to get back to work as soon as possible.

"If I'm your Shnuga Booga, then you're going to be my little minx," he said.

Lauren liked it. Davin calling her his little minx was much more appealing than him calling her Bessie. She exited the apartment while Davin held the door. He swatted her butt as she passed.

Lauren bragged, "It looks good in this skirt, doesn't it? It's the heels. They put my ass on a pedestal."

Davin smirked and shook his head side to side. It was a shame he'd have to share her for the next couple of hours.

Davin pulled into the parking lot of the Naval Media Center. He gave her a quick tour and introduced her to his colleagues. Everyone seemed friendly. Another of the sailors from their graduating class had found his way to Rota. Lauren caught up for a moment before following Davin to the radio booth. Four hours flew by as they bantered, took phone calls, played requests, and rocked out to the classics. Lauren had fun but was glad it was over. She was eager to find her new canine companions and introduce them to Davin. He loved animals as much as she did. Davin led Lauren back to his desk and left her sitting there while he checked out with his Chief. Lauren chatted with the other sailors until he returned to rescue her. He showed up just in time. She was running low on small talk and ready to leave. As they drove away from the Media Center,

Davin reported, "My Chief thinks you're really cool."

Lauren laughed. "I'm cool?" Cool was not a word she was associated with very often.

Davin continued, "You are cool. Anyway, he invited everyone out for drinks this evening at his favorite bar in honor of your visit." Lauren just wanted to spend her time with Davin.

She sighed and whined, "I don't want to hang out with people I don't know. I came here to be with you."

Davin pleaded, "Please, Lauren. We'll go for a little bit. We kind of have to go since he's letting me leave work to spend time with you while you're here." He made a good point. Lauren knew a few hours of discomfort would be worth it in the end.

"Okay, I'll go, but you can't leave me alone," she paused, "and before we leave the base, you need to stop and buy dog food."

Davin asked, "Are you going to feed me dog food for dinner?"

Lauren laughed, "No! I found some strays on the beach this morning when I was running. One of them looks like she's going to have puppies. I gave them the leftovers."

Davin joked, "Phew! I thought I was in the dog house." Davin pulled into the commissary and bought dog food while Lauren waited in the car. Then they drove to his apartment to find and feed the animals Lauren had befriended before they had to leave again.

Lauren spent her next few days in Spain sending Davin off to work and running on the beach in the mornings. Afterward, the dogs would follow her to the apartment where she'd feed them. When Davin arrived home, they would go sightseeing together. Then he'd take her out to eat, or they'd return to the apartment, and she'd cook them a meal. Afterward, they would drink wine and make love before falling asleep. Lauren had become very fond of their routine and was beginning to dread its end. She'd be going home in two days. Lauren sat on the terrace listening to the waves and thinking about how wonderful her time with Davin had been. She wasn't ready to go home. She knew Davin felt bad they hadn't done much sightseeing. When he apologized, she tried to reassure him. She never cared where they were or what they did as long as they were together.

When Davin got home, he found her on the terrace. Lauren was happy to see him. She was stuck in her head and needed a distraction. They kissed. "I have good news," he said. "I know you told me you didn't care that we didn't get to see much, but I did. I requested leave for your last days in Spain, and my Chief approved it."

Lauren was surprised. She asked, "Really?"

He went on, "Yes and it gets better. We're going to spend the whole day in Seville tomorrow. I've reserved a room near the Cathedral. We'll be close to the airport so I can get you there on time for your flight the next day."

Lauren wasn't sure what to say. She appreciated his thoughtfulness, but it also saddened her. "That means I have to pack tonight," she said. "I'd better start gathering my things."

She left Davin on the terrace and began to collect her belongings. Lauren often reverted to a robotic, task-oriented disposition as a coping mechanism. She was getting better at acknowledging and dealing with her feelings thanks to her trust in Davin and his unconditional love and support, but sometimes it seemed easier to go back to emotional evasion. She once found pride in having such a honed survival skill, but with Davin, she'd come to identify it wasn't the healthiest habit. Davin followed her into the house watching her collect her things. She silently handed him a few items, which he promptly sat down.

Lauren stopped and inquired, "Are you going to help me or not?"

Davin swept her up in his arms, carried her over to the couch, and sat down. "Will I help you go into shutdown mode? No. Do I want you to go back to Texas? Nope. Will I ever stop loving you? Never," he said.

Lauren mumbled, "No, Nope, Never."

Davin reiterated, "No, Nope, Never. However, I will help you relax. I'm making dinner tonight. We're going to have a lovely evening after I put the grill I left in the car together. We will worry about packing bags tomorrow morning before we leave and we'll do it together." Lauren laid her head on his shoulder and sighed with relief.

Davin continued, "I love you, and I'm going to make love to you now to prove it." Lauren smiled and tilted her head up to reach his lips. Intimacy always pulled her back to him. That evening Davin comforted, fed, and successfully suspended her countdown. He'd done all the things he said he would and then some. He was a man of his word and Lauren greatly appreciated every bit of his character.

The next day, Lauren and Davin drove to Seville where they left the car at the airport and took a taxi into town. After buying a tourist map from the driver, they set off on foot to find as many of the sights as possible. The city was beautiful, and the street performers who were dancing the flamenco, were extraordinary. When they were tired of walking, they hopped on a bus for a guided tour. Their last stop was the Santa Maria de la Sede Cathedral. Lauren had once read a book about it and had to see it. They roamed the halls taking in its gothic architecture and visited the tomb of explorer Christopher Columbus. The day was drawing to its end, and they were starving. Lauren and Davin found a place to eat dinner. When they'd finished, they made their way to the hotel.

While checking in Davin whispered, "It doesn't look like the pictures online."

Lauren tiredly declared, "I'm sure it will be fine." They found their room and went in. As they looked around, Lauren burst into hysterical laughter. Davin was not amused.

He said, "This is nothing like the pictures. I'm taking you someplace else." The small room was just big enough for the full sized bed it held. Lauren, still laughing, pushed open a door she thought would reveal a closet to find a tiny bathroom with a tiny bathtub.

"The tub is a miniature! Wait, this is a hostel. You brought me to a hostel!"

Davin, still visibly upset, started to smile when he saw her excitement. "This is awesome," she said.

"Now, we're real tourists." Lauren hugged and kissed him.

She continued, "You know I don't care about this kind of stuff. It's just you and me making memories now and forever."

Davin asked, "You really want to stay here?"

"Are you kidding me? We're staying," she said.

"Now, get in the bathtub so I can take a picture. I need a size reference!" Davin complied and climbed in. With his long legs crooked against his chest, Lauren began to take pictures.

She stopped and demanded, "Smile. You're frowning in my memories."

Davin removed his scowl for her and posed with a smile. When she finished, he climbed out, and they prepared for bed. Lauren and Davin could hear every little sound through the paper-thin walls.

Lauren whispered, "Davin, we probably shouldn't have sex tonight."

Davin whispered back, "Yeah, everyone would hear us. They can probably hear us whispering now."

They both crawled into bed and turned out the lights. They were drifting away in each other's embraced when they heard a man mumbling as he came down the hall. When he reached their room, he loudly released his flatulence before passing by.

Lauren and Davin quietly snickered. Davin asked, "Is it still amazing?"

Lauren responded, "This is going to be one of our favorite stories. You wait and see. Goodnight, Shnuga Booga."

He replied, "Goodnight, my little minx."

Lauren and Davin awoke a few hours later. Lauren had a very early flight, and they still needed to catch a taxi to the airport. The man at the front desk was kind and called one for them. When it arrived, they got in and made the short trip to the airport for her departure. Before she left him to go through security, Lauren made Davin promise to keep feeding the dogs she'd found. When he had assured her sufficiently, they said their usual end of visit goodbyes. Lauren wished this part would get easier, but it never seemed to. She passed through security and looked back as she always did. Davin was still there waiting to complete their ritual. After exchanging a final wave, they went their separate ways. Lauren wasn't sure when she'd see him again, but she hoped it would be soon.

Chapter 6

Lauren was exhausted from all her traveling. She'd returned from Spain without incident and reported to her April Battle Assembly. She was performing her training activities with the other soldiers when Sergeant First Class Camp came to retrieve her. Lauren followed him to the Commander's office where they all sat down.

Her commander, Major Badilla, began, "Private Mayer, I need to inform you that you were cross-leveled to a detachment in Dallas. We tried to stop it because we needed you for our deployment numbers, but since they are deploying before us, they had priority."

Lauren's heart began to pound. She asked, "Why?"

Sergeant First Class Camp chimed in, "They lost a soldier due to medical issues at the last minute. We sent you to film that ceremony for them in December, so they had your name. This is your last drill with us. Their Commander should be contacting you with your deployment orders for Operation Iraqi Freedom."

Lauren was stunned. She had been mentally prepared to deploy to Afghanistan sometime before the end of the year, but now she'd be going to Iraq and soon.

She asked, "Do you know what their mission is, sir?"

He responded, "Yes. They will take over the American Forces Network in theater."

Lauren searched her mind. In military jargon theater was short for a theater of war which just meant a region where military operations were occurring or progressing. U.S. operations in Iraq were extensive. She wished she could ask more questions but was sure her command would not have the answers due to operational security concerns. She would have to report to her new command before she could ask anything further. Even then, the information would be on a need to know basis. Lauren finished out her final Battle Assembly and was given her military personnel and medical records to hand carry to her new unit. She thanked everyone and said goodbye. When she was home, she called Davin.

Lauren cried as she spoke with him. "I have no idea what's going to happen," she said. "These people are strangers. I'm sure they're all bonded since they've been preparing together for a while. I'll be the odd man out." Davin was upset too. Neither of them was prepared for this news.

Davin comforted her, "We should try not to overthink." Davin was right. Lauren hung up the phone feeling a little better. She decided to wait until she knew more before telling Judy. Lauren prioritized her thoughts and wrote out her questions. She needed answers and contacting her new Commander was at the top of her list.

The next morning, Lauren logged into her Army information portal to locate the phone number for her new unit. She was surprised to find an email from the Commander welcoming her to the detachment.

Lauren dialed the number included in the email, and the Commander promptly answered, "Hello, this is Major Rodrick." Lauren was surprised to hear a female voice.

She replied, "Yes. This is Private Mayer. I understand I belong to you now."

Major Rodrick cheerfully responded, "Yes. Yes, you do. I'm so glad to hear from you. I'm sure you have lots of questions."

Lauren began with, "What's next, Ma'am?"

The Commander answered, "We pulled you from your unit. We are working on orders to fly you to Dallas on Wednesday. I spoke with Sergeant First Class Camp this morning. He said you have your records?"

Lauren confirmed, "Yes. I do, Ma'am."

She continued, "Good. We need them here as soon as possible, and we'd like to meet you."

Lauren asked, "What is the timeline for departure to Iraq, Ma'am?"

She responded, "You'll have approximately one month to get your affairs in order before the unit heads to Fort Polk, Louisiana for pre-deployment training. Sometime after this is complete, we'll head down range." The Commander told her to watch her email for her flight information. Lauren thanked her and assured her she would.

After hanging up, Lauren called Judy who was in class and left a message, "It's Lauren. I was going to ask when you'd be home. I'll talk to you when you get here."

Lauren left a message with Davin too when he didn't pick up, "Hey, Shnuga Booga. I talked to my new Commander. There's so much I need to do. I'm struggling today. Call me soon please. I love you. Bye."

As she was saying the last sentences, her emotions engulfed her, and she began to cry. Lauren knew he was at work. She tried to comfort herself with this thought, but knowing he'd call her back eventually didn't help how she felt now. Lauren was lost, scared, and overwhelmed. Alone and with no one to talk to, she went to the kitchen and found a bottle of wine she'd seen in the pantry. Judy's boyfriend always brought a bottle when he came over. Lauren did not know if Judy was saving it for some reason or if she would be mad if she drank it. Lauren didn't care that it wasn't even noon yet. She was upset.

As Lauren pulled it from the shelf, she said, "Finders, keepers." She opened the bottle and sat down on the cold tile of her living room floor where she drank and cried until she could not cry anymore.

Judy came home to find her passed out on the floor with the empty wine bottle next to her.

She leaned over and woke her, "Lauren. Lauren, I'm home. Wake up!" Lauren slowly opened her eyes. Finally, someone was there she could talk to.

Judy continued, "What did you do? Did you drink the whole bottle?"

Lauren replied, "I drank that," pointing at the bottle. She realized her response did not correctly match the query. She was still tipsy.

Judy retrieved a glass of water and handed it to her. "What's going on?" Lauren closed her eyes and thought hard.

She needed to form intelligible sentences. "I'm going to Iraq. I have one month to get ready."

Judy asked, "Do you want to talk about this later?" Lauren told her, "No. Let's do it now. What do you want to do about the house? Do you want to stay here?"

Lauren had signed a rent to own contract with the property owner, Mr. Arnold Hummel, before she joined the military. With all the impending uncertainty, she wasn't sure she'd made the right decision regarding homeownership at this time in her life.

She loved the place but knew Judy did a lot of driving back and forth to her college campus in San Marcos. "Cliff and I were talking the other day, and he mentioned getting a place together closer to campus," she said.

"I told him I didn't want to leave you here alone, but if you're going to Iraq, I don't want to be here alone either."

Lauren apologized, "I know. I'm sorry. I thought I had more time to worry about this stuff. I think I'm going to ask Mr. Hummel if I can terminate the contract in light of the circumstances."

Lauren sighed, "Okay I'll talk to Mr. Hummel after you talk to Cliff. We need to decide what we're doing and have it done in four weeks. Also, I have to go to Dallas on Wednesday to report to my new detachment. See, this is why I drank that."

Lauren pointed again. Judy laughed and asked, "And how do you feel now?"

Lauren complained, "Terrible. I'm going back to sleep." Lauren left the floor and headed for her bedroom. She decided to call Davin again before she fell asleep. He was laughing when he answered the phone. Lauren could hear loud conversation and commotion in the background.

She asked, "Where are you?"

Davin explained, "I'm at a bar with the guys. We came after work."

She informed him, "I called you earlier and left a message."

"I saw," he said. "I haven't listened to it yet." Lauren was instantly infuriated. She'd needed him. She was falling apart, and he was cavorting in paradise, getting drunk with his friends.

"You chose to ignore me? I know you don't have a care in the world, but I do. I have all the cares, and I needed to talk to my best friend," she said.

Lauren could feel her shut down coming. "There's no point in calling you or leaving you a message telling you I need you. There's no reason for me to be your girlfriend or to be vulnerable for that matter if you're not going to answer or listen or care. You blew me off for beers," she screamed.

The noise dissipated and Davin responded, "I'm sorry, Lauren. I walked outside to talk to you."

Davin had never done this to her before. Lauren had always been a priority. She'd gotten used to being treated like the most important thing in his world, and right now she wasn't.

Lauren dejectedly said, "I don't want to talk anymore. I'll just cry again, and then there will be snot. I'm sorry I interrupted your fun."

Davin urged, "Lauren, I'm here."

"You're not though," she said. "You're ready to pacify me and get back to your friends. My feelings are extremely hurt. I'm hanging up."

Davin apologized again, "I'm sorry, sweetheart. I love you. I'll call you before I go to bed."

She responded, "Okay. I love you too. Bye." Lauren hung up the phone. She and Davin had argued about silly things before, but this was the first time he'd truly hurt her feelings. She wondered if maybe she was overly sensitive. After all, she was impaired and emotionally overwrought. She reminded herself Davin would never hurt her on purpose, as she closed her tear-filled eyes and fell asleep.

Lauren awoke to her phone ringing. It was Davin calling as promised. She was glad they'd ended their call before. She was a mess and needed time to rest, sober up, and compartmentalize. Lauren knew she didn't have control over anything in her life except her behavior and emotions. It was imperative she regulate them. Feelings were annoying anyway and made her vulnerable. Moreover, she would be headed into a war zone. A soft soldier was a bad one, and she did not want to be a liability.

After letting it ring a few times, Lauren answered the phone, "Hello."

"Sweetheart, I am sorry. I listened to your message, and I'm sorry I wasn't there for you," Davin said.

Lauren knew he had a life half a world away from her. "It's okay. You're allowed to do what you want with your time. I was upset earlier. I'm trying to process everything, and I miss you. I'm sorry too. I shouldn't have yelled at you," she said.

Lauren and Davin made up. She could never stay mad at him for long anyway. She loved him too much. They exchanged sweet nothings until both felt reassured in their relationship and hung up pleased they'd navigated this bump properly. Still in bed, Lauren grabbed the journal and pen she kept in her bedside table. She started a to-do list. At the top, she wrote as she said aloud, "Do not drink. It makes you squishy." Lauren continued writing until she'd finished her list. On paper, it all seemed doable. Lauren decided she would begin to conquer her tasks the next day and settled into her pillows to watch a film. Judy came into her room to talk, so Lauren paused the movie.

"I spoke with Cliff, and we're going apartment hunting tomorrow," she said.

"Alright then," Lauren responded. "I don't want to talk about that stuff anymore today. Come watch with me."

Judy joined her, and they ordered a pizza. Comedy, food, and company were the remedy Lauren needed. She and Judy stayed up late even though she was tired. Lauren was glad she had her sister to comfort her and grateful for the distraction.

The next day, Lauren awoke feeling rested and ready to tackle anything. It was a beautiful morning, and she was determined to make the best of it. Lauren ripped her list from the journal. Her first task was to call Mr. Hummel.

When he answered, she began, "Hi, this is Lauren Mayer. May I speak with Mr. Hummel?" When he'd confirmed he was speaking, Lauren went on, "Mr. Hummel, I have an issue that's arisen. I'm deploying to Iraq." Lauren explained she did not know how long the deployment would last, but if current rumors were true, she'd be gone for more than a year. She told him Judy did not want to be there alone and that the house would be empty. After she informed him of the improvements she'd made, she asked,

"Would it be possible to terminate our agreement in light of this development?" Mr. Hummel reminisced about his own service. Lauren didn't know he was a veteran.

After chatting a while, Mr. Hummel agreed to release her from the obligation saying, "I understand. I'll need a copy of your orders, and I'll need to inspect the house."

Lauren sat down at the dining room table and added this to her list."

He continued, "I'm so sad to see you go. I'll have my attorney draft the documents we'll need to sign." Lauren heard a knock at the door. Still on the phone with Mr. Hummel, she left the dining room table to answer the door. It was a deliveryman with a bouquet of two dozen, long-stemmed, red roses. Lauren thanked Mr. Hummel and wrapped up her conversation.

After she hung up the phone, she addressed the deliveryman, "I'm sorry."

"That's okay," he said.

"Are you, Lauren Mayer?" Lauren confirmed she was and took the bouquet from him. She shut the door with her foot as he left. They flowers were heavy. She quickly walked them back to the dining room where she set them on the table. They were stunning. Lauren had never received an arrangement this large.

She pulled the card from the middle and read, *"Lauren, I know you've had a rough couple of days. Everything will be okay. You always make me feel like a king when I'm down. Today it's my turn to make you feel better. My queen, your smile is worth every single one of these roses and more. Keep smiling and remember I love you. Sincerely, Your King, Davin."*

Lauren felt blessed to have such a wonderful man in her life. She replaced the card and picked up her list from the table. Lauren decided to call Davin to thank him for the flowers. She also wanted to let him know she'd be returning the house and putting her things into storage. After, she would pack for her trip to Dallas to meet her new command. Lauren hung onto Davin's words. In her world, everything needed to be okay. She'd just have to keep reminding herself it would be.

Lauren made the flight from San Antonio to Dallas where she rented a car and drove to the Army reserve post to meet her new Commander. When she arrived at the detachment, she reported to Major Wanda Rodrick's office. She was a tall, thin, redhead who greeted her cordially with a copy of her deployment orders. Major Rodrick introduced her to a few of the other soldiers who were there including her Section Sergeant, Sergeant First Class Gene Edmundson. Sergeant First Class Edmundson looked as though he was in his late sixties, wore a wedding band, and had a gray horseshoe hairline. He reeked of cigarettes and coffee and leaned in uncomfortably close when speaking. There was something about him Lauren did not particularly care for. She wasn't sure what it was, but his disregard of her personal space certainly did not help. In all the new faces Lauren was happy to see a familiar one. One of the students she knew from Fort Meade would be deploying too. He was a technical engineer named Clay Longmire. He had also been one of the members of her marathon relay team. She and Private Longmire had always been friendly. They weren't close, but they had spent several months training together and going to school for their respective specialties. Lauren didn't feel so much like an outsider anymore. She and Longmire spent the remainder of the day catching up and filling out deployment paperwork in the detachment's studio. Sergeant First Class Edmundson interrupted them periodically to check on their progress. When Lauren had finished with her stack of documents, she left Longmire and returned to the office. The administrative sergeant was not there, but Sergeant First Class Edmundson was.

He asked, "Are you done?"

Lauren replied, "Yes, Sergeant." Sergeant First Class Edmundson stood from where he was sitting and walked over to review her paperwork. As he was going through the pile, he stopped and leaned in even closer than he already was.

He took a deep breath and commented, "You smell amazing."

She was quickly beginning to realize this man was predatory. Sergeant First Class Edmundson continued, "You and Longmire seem like you're really good friends." Lauren felt like he was insinuating their friendship was more than just a friendship.

Trying to figure out where this conversation was going she said, "We're friends."

He continued, "So you know, I heard Longmire talking about you with another soldier and he said you were a skank." Lauren had spent time with Longmire and had never heard him talk that way about anyone.

Lauren responded, "I don't believe Longmire said that, especially about me." As Lauren was finishing her sentence, Longmire walked into the office to return his paperwork. He had overheard Sergeant First Class Edmundson talking about him as he approached and decided to listen and wait just outside the doorway.

Now standing next to her, Longmire said, "I have never called Mayer a skank. I didn't even know she was deploying with us until she arrived today and I've spent the whole day with her in the studio filling out paperwork. I've hardly spoken to anyone else to call her names, Sergeant."

Lauren was glad someone else was in the room. She did not care for this man at all now. He had just lied for an obvious ulterior motive and been caught. Sergeant First Class Edmundson laughed it off and left them standing in the office together.

Lauren looked over at Longmire and asked, "What's his deal?"

Longmire warned her, "Watch out for him. He's a perv." With that, they went in search of the admin sergeant to turn in their documents. After checking out with the Major, Lauren returned to her hotel room for the night. She would be leaving the next day. Lauren was repacking her luggage and watching television when she heard a knock at her door. She looked through the peephole to see Sergeant First Class Edmundson. Lauren opened the door and said, "Hello, Sergeant Edmundson."

"Hello," he said.

"Would you like to join me for dinner?"

Lauren did not think this was a good idea, so she declined saying, "No thank you. I'm not hungry."

He asked, "How about drinks then?" Lauren desperately wanted to close her door, but she needed to be respectful. This man was her first resource in the detachment's chain of command.

She informed him, "I'm not twenty-one, Sergeant." Sergeant First Class Edmundson took offense at her rejection.

He abruptly stated, "Fine. The real reason I came by is to tell you I have a copy of your orders."

Lauren felt incredibly uncomfortable, but went on as nicely as possible, "I have a copy of them, Sergeant. The Major gave them to me this morning. Thank you. Have a lovely evening."

She quickly closed the door and locked all the locks. Earlier, Lauren had read the Commander's open-door policy regarding problems that were private in nature or issues with someone in the chain of command. Lauren thought this man might be an issue in the future, so she wrote a quick email to the Major regarding his behavior. If she were going to have to deal with Sergeant First Class Edmundson indefinitely, she wanted to make sure his conduct was documented in case he escalated. Lauren sent her email and started another. She addressed this one to Davin. She wrote him all about her day and promised to call him when she was home. Then she went to bed.

The following day, Lauren arrived home to her beautiful flowers. Now she had less than three and a half weeks to get her things in order and she knew they would go by quickly.

Stressed, she phoned Davin who answered lovingly. "Hey baby." His voice was soothing.

Lauren responded, "Hi, Shnuga."

"I got your email about that pervert," he said.

Lauren countered, "It was bizarre. I don't like the guy. I don't think Longmire likes him."

Davin replied, "I don't like either of them."

Lauren laughed and asked, "What did Longmire ever do to you?"

Davin continued, "Nothing. I just think you're beautiful and if I believe it, he does too. I know people bond in stressful situations."

Lauren reassured him, "Please don't worry. Longmire and I are just friends. You are my lover. I don't want to be with anyone else, stress or no stress. I miss you. I wish you were here. I have so much to do and so little time."

Davin responded, "I will be."

Confused Lauren asked, "You will be what?"

Davin announced, "I'll be there to help you with whatever you need help with. I wanted to surprise you, but I can't keep a secret."

"You're coming here? When," she asked.

"I requested leave. I told my Chief you were deploying and he approved it. Anyway, I'll fly in on Monday and stay for two weeks. You didn't think I was going to let you run off to a war zone without a proper goodbye, did you?" That is exactly what Lauren thought, but she was glad it would not be so.

Davin asked, "Are you excited?" Lauren happily confessed,

"Yes. Of course, I'm excited. Now I can wait until you get here and make you do everything!"

Davin joked, "Don't push it. I'm not on the plane yet!"

"I am going to wait until you get here to start the moving process though," she said.

"I think I might spend some time with my family. I don't know when I'll be able to if I don't do it this weekend."

He replied, "Sounds good sweetheart. They're going to miss you too."

Lauren and Davin said goodbye so Lauren could do her laundry before leaving again. All she did was travel. She was glad she and Mr. Hummel had come to an agreement about the house. She would be signing it back over to him when he came to inspect it. The house didn't feel like her home anymore. It had become a place for her to sleep like any other hotel room or barracks bed. Everything was changing fast. As Lauren locked the doors to leave for the weekend, she redirected her thoughts to her current mission. *"Let's go Lauren,"* she said.

Lauren's family lived in a typical tiny Texas town named Walnut Springs. It was quiet and relaxed compared to where Lauren lived, and she was enjoying every bit of it. While her parents' barbequed, she played with her little brother and sister. Later, Lauren caught everyone up on her life, her plans, and her limited deployment information. Even though the undertone of the weekend was worry, they all made the best of their time together.

As Lauren packed her car to return to New Braunfels, her mother asked, "Can you stay a little longer?"

Lauren replied, "I wish I could, but I have a lot to do. I need to pack and get my things in storage. My boyfriend, Davin, is coming to help me. Maybe you can finally meet him."

Lauren hugged everyone and promised, "I'll be back to visit before I leave for good."

Lauren got in her car and waved as she pulled away. The drive back felt like an impossibly long one especially since she was alone with her thoughts. She was glad when she finally pulled back into her driveway. As she entered the garage, she saw a sea of boxes.

Lauren went in and found Judy. "Did you find a place?" she asked.

"Yes, we did," replied Judy.

Lauren spotted Cliff on the floor in the corner of the room and said, "Well, congratulations!"

Judy was excited, "It's really cute and close to campus. I should be moved in by the end of the week.

"That's great," said Lauren. "Davin is flying in today. I'm picking him up later." Lauren looked down at her watch realizing the time. She had been so distracted by her mind she'd lost track. She needed to leave as soon as possible if there were any hope of welcoming him at the terminal.

Judy responded, "Okay, we probably won't be here when you get back. This is our last trip for the day." Lauren finished her conversation and left for the airport. She crossed her fingers in hopes that his flight might be delayed.

On the way, she called Davin and left a message, "Baby, I'm so sorry. I'm running late. You're probably landing right now. I'll be there in thirty minutes." Lauren felt terrible as she sped down the highway. Not only was she breaking the law, but she wouldn't be there to greet Davin when he arrived. Lauren was maneuvering in and out of traffic when Davin returned her call.

"Lauren, where are you? Did you forget me," he asked.

Lauren responded, "Of course not. I'm taking the exit for the airport now. I'll pick you up outside the terminal?"

Davin agreed, and Lauren hung up. She pulled up alongside the curb of the terminal where she saw him waiting with his luggage parked next to him and his arms crossed. Any irritation quickly turned to joy when she jumped out of the car to hug him.

As she kissed him, she said, "I promise I'll make this up to you. Anything you want!"

Davin laughed and asked, "Anything? I have a few ideas."

"Really," she replied sarcastically.

"Yes, really. Let's go. We'll need some privacy," he said with a wink. Lauren kissed him again, and they both got into the car to make their way back to her house.

The next two weeks were a whirlwind of organizing, packing, cleaning and preparing the house for its return to Mr. Hummel. Lauren and Davin stole as many intimate moments as they could between it all. After Judy had finished her move, they had all the privacy they needed to enjoy each other thoroughly, and they did. After signing Mr. Hummel's papers, Lauren and Davin made the trip to Walnut Springs to put her things into storage. They spent a few days with her family. Lauren's mother and father liked him immensely, but had rules and did not allow them to sleep in the same room while they were visiting. Davin was given her brother's room and Lauren slept on the couch.

On the morning of his departure, Lauren snuck into the room where he was sleeping and woke him. They silently made love to each other beneath the covers. This would be the last time they could be intimate for months and they both desperately needed the connection. As always, he felt amazing. It was difficult for Lauren to remain quiet, but she had to. As he rhythmically stroked her, Lauren thought the silence truly was golden. While they were holding back on erotic verbal encouragement, they were not on passionate visual cues and sensual caresses. Their level of intimacy greatly intensified with their indulgence in their other senses. As they both reached climax, Lauren fought against her desire to break her silence. When they had finished, she quietly remained in his arms as long as she could. They were both hot under the blanket that had concealed the sexual pleasures of their committed relationship. Neither one of them cared that they were sticky with the sweat of their accomplishment or that their skin had seemingly melted together.

Lauren watched the clock wishing its second hand would stop ticking. She wanted time to stand still, but dawn would be arriving soon as would dusk. Every passing tick was a cadence to her march toward inevitable departure to Iraq. Lauren kissed Davin, and they quietly exchanged sweet nothings before she returned to the living room. Her remaining days were fewer and fewer, and it was becoming more difficult for her to remain collected with each passing one. Inside Lauren was a puddle of emotions, but felt it vital to maintain an unperturbed façade for Davin and her family. If they knew how scared she truly was, they'd be terrified as well. Fear would not comfort anyone. Lauren knew she was a soldier. In the still of the room and low light of the first rays peaking from the horizon, she realized she had reached a place of acceptance. She was ready to complete her mission with confidence, and if she ever waivered, even a little, she would just tell herself, *"Everything will be okay."*

Chapter 7

Lauren leaned on a bus in the detachment's parking lot watching the other soldiers say goodbye to their families and friends. She'd said her goodbyes to Davin the week before and to her family the day before when they dropped her off at a nearby hotel. She was glad they weren't there. The tears and the hugs were almost too much to bear. When the chaplain arrived, they all gathered and held hands to say a prayer before departing. Since they were a Reserve Unit, they would need to complete pre-deployment training at Fort Polk, Louisiana before being sent to Kuwait and then on to Iraq. The Commander announced it was time to leave and after a head count, the bus pulled away from the remaining loved ones.

The trip to Fort Polk was somber. The soldiers hardly spoke to one another until they pulled onto the base. When they stopped and dismounted in front of their barracks, suddenly everyone had something to share. Lauren sat quietly listening to the complaints and banter. It appeared World War II era wooden buildings would be their home for the duration of their stay. It was summertime and hot. Lauren knew these structures would provide little comfort in the way of air-conditioning; then again, they were headed to the desert. The objective here was combat training and clearly, no time would be wasted on comfort.

The mission of the Joint Readiness Training Center at Fort Polk was to provide soldiers with realistic conditions for sensitivity and tactical training. Every day there was a new unit-based mission, which incorporated team building and operation essential exercises. Lauren had just done all this at basic training, but it hadn't been with this group of people. Some of the others needed the refresher. Even though it was exhausting, Lauren was glad to have this opportunity to get to know the rest of the detachment's soldiers. As the weeks passed and the training exercises were checked off, the Commander announced each of the section Sergeants would be performing individual evaluations. Lauren knew this meant one on one time with Sergeant First Class Edmundson. She'd become practiced at avoiding and deflecting his inappropriate conduct. Now she'd be forced to sit in front of him and carry on a conversation.

One day, following a training exercise, Sergeant First Class Edmundson approached her and said, "Private Mayer, I need to meet with you to conduct your counseling."

Lauren replied, "Yes, Sergeant."

Sergeant First Class Edmundson continued, "Meet me in the wood line by the barracks after dinner."

Lauren was taken aback but again responded, "Yes, Sergeant."

Lauren did not want to meet with this man in the wood line after sunset. It was grossly inappropriate. Lauren was not sure what to do. If she didn't go, she'd be disobeying an order and did not want to be written up for insubordination. This man already had too much power over her. She wasn't about to give him more. Lauren thought about it and decided to talk to the female Sergeant in her section. She'd never talked to Sergeant Caitlin Cole before. She was blonde, sarcastic, and at times had a biting wit. Once Longmire had told her, Sergeant Cole served in an active duty capacity before joining the reserves. Lauren thought she might be able to give her some advice.

A few minutes before she was supposed to report, Lauren approached her. "Sergeant Cole, may I talk to you?" she asked.

"Yeah, I guess," replied Cole. Lauren told her about Sergeant First Class Edmundson's previous sexual harassment. She also told her about him ordering her to the wood line.

Sergeant Cole was skeptical and replied, "No way. The wood line for counseling? Did you do something?" Lauren was a stranger to her, and while it was plausible this could have been a punishment, the reality was she hadn't done anything wrong.

Lauren assured her, "I haven't done anything."

Sergeant Cole inquired again, "Are you sure?"

A female Sergeant from another section overhead their conversation and stepped in saying, "She shouldn't be meeting him alone in the wood line for any reason. That shit is crazy. You need to go with her, Cole."

Sergeant Cole sighed heavily. Lauren knew attending this counseling was the last thing she wanted to do, but she was relieved.

"When do you have to go," Cole asked.

"Right now," answered Lauren.

Sergeant Cole irritably said, "Well, let's go."

When Lauren and Sergeant Cole arrived at the wood line, they found Sergeant First Class Edmundson waiting.

He asked, "What are you doing here Sergeant Cole?"

Sergeant Cole responded, "Private Mayer was uncomfortable with this arrangement and brought it to my attention."

Lauren added, "I asked Sergeant Cole to accompany me." Sergeant First Class Edmondson was visibly angry.

He yelled, "You have not obeyed my order."

Lauren countered, "I did, Sergeant. I reported as requested."

He screamed again, "You are insubordinate, and for that, you will be written up."

Sergeant Cole interrupted, "She's here. Private Mayer has not been insubordinate. She was obviously justified in questioning your intentions here. You didn't perform any of the other female soldier's reviews out in the wood line. Perform hers, so we get back and report your inappropriate behavior to the Commander."

Lauren was glad there was a witness to this man's latest scheme in sexual harassment. Sergeant First Class Edmundson finished his counseling and stormed off. Lauren and Sergeant Cole stood looking at each other in disbelief. Lauren was not prepared for his level of fury at her thwarting of whatever plan he'd devised.

Lauren acknowledged, "He's pissed."

Sergeant Cole responded, "We need to talk to the Commander. I didn't believe you. How long has this been going on?" As they walked back to the barracks, Lauren recalled some of the incidents.

She also told her, "The Commander knows about it. I've documented it all. I don't know if she doesn't care or if she has too much on her plate. Anyway, thank you."

Sergeant Cole assured her, "We'll make sure she knows about this too. I've never seen anything like that before, and I've been doing this awhile. Hopefully, it won't happen again."

They arrived back at the barracks and after talking to the Commander went their separate ways. Lauren called Davin to vent.

He answered excitedly, "Hey Baby!" She was happy to hear his voice. She told him all about what had happened.

Davin comforted her saying, "I'm so sorry you have to deal with that guy. You don't deserve to be treated that way." Lauren thanked him.

He asked her, "Do you want to hear something that will cheer you up?"

Lauren replied, "Yes!"

"The momma dog finally had her puppies. I went to feed them, and the puppies were there under a cactus thicket," he reported. "I dug them all out. There are six boys and one girl. I'm going to work on finding the boys, momma, and daddy homes. I think I might keep the girl."

Lauren was glad to hear this. She responded, "Good! A puppy will keep you company. What are you going to name her?"

"I don't know," he said. "Help me think of something." Lauren needed the distraction and started suggesting some names.

Davin shot down every one saying, "Those are too girly."

"She's a girl," retorted Lauren. "What about Tallulah?"

Davin repeated, "Tallulah. It's too long, but Lula would work."

He directed his next comment to the puppy. "Do you like the name, Lula?" Lauren laughed and waited.

"Yup! Her name is Lula. She likes it." Davin always made Lauren feel better. She wasn't sure how she'd make it without him by her side, but she was determined to get through it so she could be back in her sailor's arms.

As Lauren and her unit finished the last days of training, word came there was a tropical storm named Katrina in the Gulf of Mexico. The Joint Readiness Training Center had been keeping track of its development. Concern began when the National Weather Service updated the storm's status to a hurricane. Shortly after, a state of emergency was declared in the state of Louisiana. The Commander ordered the detachment to prepare for a swift departure ahead of its landfall. Once she received the go-ahead from her superiors, the unit was mobilized for transport overseas.

When the group finally landed at the Ali Al Salem Air Base in Kuwait, they were transferred to Camp Buehring. A military liaison took them to a chow hall to eat breakfast. There they watched news reports of the devastation from Katrina's landfall. Lauren could not believe how surreal it felt to be sitting approximately twenty-five miles from the Iraqi border looking at images of destruction from a state she'd been in forty-eight hours before. The group was not done traveling though. After they ate, they were loaded onto a C-130 to Baghdad International Airport. When they arrived, they waited until dark for transport on a bus, which resembled an armored Winnebago named the Rhino. The Rhino Runner staged for departure at varying times of night due to operational security. Once the Apache helicopters arrived to provide air support, the detachment and any others waiting to depart were escorted down the infamous Route Irish to the Green Zone.

At their destination, the Republican Palace, they were eagerly greeted by the outgoing detachment. There would be a few days of cross training before they officially took over the Baghdad based news program Freedom Journal Iraq and the American Forces Network - Iraq radio broadcasts. Until then, they would process into the country and recover from their exhausting journey.

Lauren was happy to be given temporary quarters to sleep, but also eager to be assigned something more permanent. She was also ready to talk to Davin. He knew to expect silence from her when it was time for her to move out. Davin understood how a mobilization worked from his own military experience. She missed him though and anxiously wanted to talk to him. It was the one-year anniversary of the day they'd met and first shook hands in a classroom at Fort Meade. Also, her birthday, September fifth, was just five days away. It should have been a happy time. She and Davin should have been celebrating their first anniversary together. Lauren tried to comfort herself with the thought that in Iraq she was closer to him than she had been in the United States, but it wasn't nearly as reassuring as she had hoped. Lauren didn't know when she'd have an opportunity to call him, so she wrote him a letter before falling asleep. There'd be lots to do when the sun rose, and she needed to rest.

Major Rodrick woke her female soldiers for a meeting. She started, "We are getting our trailer assignments. I'd prefer we stay together as much as possible. The trailers are set up for four people. They're modified shipping containers with two rooms—one on each end—and a shared bathroom in the middle. Please discuss it. We will be going to housing in a bit."

She left them to deliver the same news to the male soldiers who were waiting in separate temporary quarters. Lauren sat and watched as everyone paired up.

Sergeant Cole announced, "I'm going to see enough of you people at work. I don't want to see you in my spare time too so, don't ask me." Even though Lauren had found a friend in Longmire, she still felt like an outcast among the female soldiers. They were all nice, but she'd been a latecomer, and they'd already established their preferences in roommates. That left Lauren by herself and while she understood Sergeant Cole's argument, she didn't want to be further separated from the group than she already was. Lauren still didn't know Sergeant Cole very well but felt like she was someone she could get along with.

"Sergeant Cole," she said, "If you change your mind, I need a roommate."

Sergeant Cole laughed and said, "What did I just say?"

"I know," said Lauren. "But I mostly keep to myself, I'm organized, and I have good hygiene." Lauren was trying to sell herself.

She continued, "Look, you don't bother me, and I won't bother you. Besides, the Major wants us to stay together. Think about it."

When the time came for the Major to finalize the housing roster, Sergeant Cole agreed to be Lauren's roommate. She and Sergeant Cole were assigned trailer 143 Right while two other female soldiers, Specialists Jessica Cotton and Melissa Gray, were assigned 143 Left. Cotton was from California. She came complete with a laid-back, mellow personality. Gray seemed more like a curious, social butterfly. Lauren was content with the living arrangement since she got along with everyone.

One day while the four of them walked through the chow hall together, Specialist Gray spotted a soldier in line and called out to him, "Sergeant Chrisman!"

He turned to acknowledge his name and recognized her immediately.

"Hello, Specialist Gray," he said.

Specialist Gray introduced Lauren, Cotton, and Cole to Sergeant Shane Chrisman.

He inquired, "Where are you staying?"

Specialist Gray responded, "We're in trailer 143."

"Really? Welcome to the neighborhood. I'm a few down from you in 131," he said. He ended the conversation by volunteering to give them a tour later that evening. After eating and returning to the trailer, Specialist Gray asked if anyone wanted to accompany her. Cotton and Cole declined. Lauren agreed to go. She and Gray found Sergeant Chrisman at his trailer. He'd been at the Republican Palace for a while and knew the place very well. He told them all about his assignment as the General's driver as he gave them the tour, which included a stop at the palace's phone center. They'd have access to the internet soon, but until then Lauren could talk to Davin here.

When the tour was over, Sergeant Chrisman led them to the pool on the palace grounds. Contractors had turned it into a location for people to come and relax. There they were introduced to Sergeant Chrisman's roommate, Sergeant John Peters, who was invested in a game of cards. Sergeant Peters was a handsome young man, with vibrant green eyes, long eyelashes, and a chiseled jaw. Lauren immediately identified a "God's gift to women" persona with the first few words out of his mouth.

He reminded her of the character Gaston from the story Beauty and the Beast. As he played, Peters switched between the topics of his strengths and accomplishments to the stupidity of his ex-girlfriend. His arrogant chatter and self-adulation were annoying. Lauren could not take his commentary any longer.

"Do you even hear yourself when you speak?" she asked disgustedly.

"Who are you trying to impress? I hope it's not me. If it's Gray, I hope she sees right through the hot air you're rigorously pumping into your ego. Also, for your information, speaking poorly about the female gender in front of two you're actively trying to impress is completely offensive. Good Lord, I cannot listen to you anymore. Sorry, Gray. I'm out of here."

Lauren stood to leave. As she walked away, Peters hollered, "I'd say it was nice to meet you but it wasn't. I'm not interested in comments from the peanut gallery anyway!"

Lauren rolled her eyes and thought of Davin. She was so thankful his personality was nothing like Peters. Lauren made her way back to the call center and found a free phone. She sat down and dialed.

When Davin answered, she replied, "It's so nice to hear your voice."

Davin responded, "It is nice to hear you too. I was starting to worry about you."

Lauren couldn't divulge the details of her travels, but she did tell him, "Getting here was rough. It's been a crazy experience so far. There's this loudspeaker on the grounds of the compound. When there's incoming fire a siren goes off, and a voice comes on instructing us to take cover. I think it might be the voice of God."

They both laughed. "Happy anniversary, Shnuga Booga," she said.

"I wish we could talk longer, but I've got to go. There's a line. I'll send you my address soon. I love you."

"Happy anniversary, Lauren," he responded.

"Hang in there. I love you too. Bye, sweetheart."

Lauren hung up the phone and went back to her trailer to unpack. It would be her home for the next year, and she wanted to make it comfortable. Sergeant Cole had fallen asleep. Quietly, Lauren finished unpacking her things before settling in for the night.

The next day Lauren and Cole prepared for their first day at work. There was a knock at the door.

Lauren answered to find Cotton and Gray.

Cotton asked, "You guys ready?"

Lauren turned to Cole and inquired, "You ready?"

Cole confirmed she was. Lauren looked back at Gray and replied, "We're ready!"

Gray pointed to a folded piece of paper taped to the door and said, "I think you have a note."

Lauren pulled the note from the door inquiring, "Why would I have a note? Maybe it's for Cole."

"No. It's for you," said Gray.

"Sergeant Peter's asked which side you were on after you left last night. I think he felt bad."

Sergeant Cole and Specialist Cotton gave Lauren a hard time as they exited the trailer.

Sergeant Cole said, "I thought you have a boyfriend. I saw his pictures on the wall."

Cotton chimed in with, "We've been here one day, and you already have a second boyfriend. Dang!" The teasing embarrassed Lauren. She laughed and put the note in her pocket. They made their way to the office and started their day. There was a lot of information to take in and the time passed quickly.

Before dismissing the detachment for the day, Major Rodrick called a meeting. "I need two volunteers to answer the media inquiries overnight."

She explained, "All you'll have to do is answer phones and provide previously approved public affairs information." Lauren and Cotton were sitting next to each other. Cotton had married her husband right before they left Texas. Lauren had an idea and thought she too might have a personal interest in it.

She leaned toward her and whispered, "If international calls are coming in, then we can make international calls out, right? Also, we'd have the day off tomorrow."

Cotton whispered back, "No line and privacy."

Cotton quickly raised her hand declaring, "Private Mayer and I volunteer." Lauren nodded her head in agreement.

That night Lauren was finally able to talk to her family. She also called Davin. It was nice to speak with her loved ones without feeling rushed to pass the phone to the next person waiting in line. Lauren was surprised it had been such a quiet night. They'd only answered a few inquiries. After Cotton had finished her calls, she and Lauren got to know each other better. Eventually, they tired of conversation and decided to take shifts sleeping. Cotton would rest first and then Lauren. While Cotton slept, Lauren waited for the next inquiry, wandered around the internet, sent emails, and caught up on news. Running out of thing to occupy her, she looked up at the clock and began to count the hours she'd been awake.

Suddenly, she remembered the note in her pocket. Lauren pulled it out, unfolded, and began to read it.

Sergeant Peters wrote, "I'm sorry if I came across like a jerk. I'm going through a lot personally. That doesn't excuse my behavior. If you haven't noticed, the ratio of men to women is disproportionate. I've gotten pretty rough around my edges. Sincerely, Sergeant John Peters."

Lauren sighed and re-folded the letter. She had noticed there were far more men than women around. Even in her unit of twenty-seven people, there were only ten women. Lauren thought about their exchange the night before. She'd also been rude when she admonished him for being an offensive jackass in front of a group she didn't know. Lauren decided she didn't have to talk to him or like him, but she would be more cautious with her tongue. After all, Peters had apologized. Surely that meant he wasn't all pompous bravado.

As time went on and the handoff of the station was complete, the detachment settled into its mission. The radio DJ's ran the radio, while the broadcasters rotated in and out of the station on assignments collecting stories for the news broadcast, Freedom Journal Iraq. Any broadcaster sent out on a mission was gone for a week or so. They hopped helicopters, C-130's, and convoys all over the country chasing down leads. Once they had their stories, they'd do the same leapfrog to get back to the station.

Lauren always carried a satellite phone in case of an emergency. Even though she had it, Lauren rarely had the chance to speak with Davin while out on a mission and hated it. She liked being in the Green Zone since that's where she could pick up her mail or talk to him. One day, Lauren received an assignment located in the International Zone. She was excited. After gathering her equipment, Lauren made her way to the Italian compound. She would be doing a feel-good piece on Italy's role in the Multi-National Force-Iraq or the Coalition Force as it was often referred to. Lauren toured the compound, conducted interviews, and recorded video for her story. She met several individuals including an Italian NATO Officer from the Allied Joint Force Command in Naples, Italy. He was part of the NATO Training Mission. With a translator, Lieutenant Raffaele Renzo explained how he traveled to Iraqi Security Force stations within the International Zone. His team was tasked to provide training and mentoring in an effort to develop an effective and sustainable Iraqi Security Force. Lauren completed her assignment, exchanged contact information, and thanked everyone she'd worked with for their time. As she was leaving, Lauren was given an invitation from the Italian Ambassador to attend an event on the compound that evening. She thanked them again and left confident she'd gotten a great story.

When Lauren returned to her trailer, she found Cole and Cotton watching television. Cotton and Gray were on the rocks. Lauren had suspected their personalities would clash due to the difference in their natures. However, Cotton and Cole were very similar and had become close. Lauren told them about her day and handed the invitation to Cole. She was glad when they decided to go. Lauren would have the room all to herself to video chat with Davin, which she did before falling asleep. It was very late when Lauren awoke to her phone ringing. An accented voice informed her two American Forces Network journalists were intoxicated and requested she retrieve them. Alcohol consumption was prohibited under General Order Number One, and Lauren did not want them to get in trouble. She got up and quickly dressed in a pair of her Army physical fitness uniform shorts and t-shirt. On her way out the door, Lauren grabbed her shoulder holster and nine-millimeter handgun instead of her M-16. She made her way on foot to the Italian compound. When she arrived, she was directed to Cole's location. She was discussing the war and politics with the Ambassador. Lauren thanked the Italian Ambassador, apologized, and took her by the hand to find Cotton. Lauren located Cotton dancing with an Italian soldier in an open hall area.

She released Cole's hand to squeeze between the dancing partners. Lauren, speaking loudly over the music, said, "We need to go."

Cotton kept dancing. It was obvious neither one of them was ready to leave. Thankfully, the song ended. Lauren grabbed Cotton's hand and led her off the dance floor. She quickly realized Cole was gone. Cotton sat down in an empty chair while Lauren scanned the room in vain.

She instructed, "Wait here." Lauren's frustration mounted as she exited the building into a courtyard. She thought Cole might have gone outside to smoke. As she looked around, she noticed a small patch of grass. Lauren had not seen grass in some time. She was amazed at how lush and green it was. She could not help herself. Lauren quickly took off her socks and shoes, stepped into the cool blades, and wiggled her toes. Her frustration was easing away when she saw someone exit the building and approach her. She recognized him from before. It was Lieutenant Renzo.

Lauren knew he wouldn't understand, but as he came toward her she asked, "Have you seen my friend?"

Lauren thought a moment and continued, "Donna? Americana?" Lieutenant Renzo, now standing very close, attempted to kiss her. Lauren backed away inadvertently placing herself close to a gray cinder block wall. Lieutenant Renzo began speaking in Italian.

His body language was aggressive and his tone hostile. Lauren realized she was in a terrible situation. "I'm sorry," she said as she attempted to side-step him.

He quickly blocked her. Lauren had her weapon but did not want to make matters worse. This man was a NATO Officer, and her roommates were intoxicated. The last thing Lauren wanted was to be involved in an international incident. Every step she took to avoid his proximity he matched like a predator toying with his prey. Lauren was against the wall when he ran his fingers up into her hair. He gathered a handful and yanked it before smacking her hard against the wall. Lauren's head hit so forcefully she saw stars. She was desperately trying to regain her composure when he shoved his hand into her underwear and pulled hard at her pubic hair. He pressed the full weight of his body against her torso pinning her right arm. Lauren struggled to free herself, but she was no match for his strength. While slobbering all over her neck, he scratched at her privates with his fingernails. Lauren realized he was probing her crotch in search of her vagina's opening.

Lauren pleaded, "Please don't do this." Viciously, he thrust several fingers inside her digitally penetrating Lauren's vagina. His disgusting nails cut and tore at her delicate lining. Lauren cried out in pain. As he continued to assault her, she prayed, *"Please God get me through this."* Lauren gathered her strength and attempted to free herself once more. This angered him. He pulled his hand from her shorts and raised it to strike her. Lauren turned her cheek and closed her eyes tightly bracing for the blow.

Unexpectedly, she heard a male voice chanting, 'Renzo Rhino, Renzo Rhino'. Lauren opened her eyes. There was a spectator in a dark corner of the courtyard. He was smoking and apparently enjoying the violent spectacle. Lauren didn't know how long he'd been watching. Lieutenant Renzo suddenly stopped what he was doing. With a smirk, he slowly lifted his weight off her and took a few steps back. Lauren was not sure if she should be relieved someone had interrupted the assault with his gleeful cheering or if she should prepare for more brutality. Lauren shifted her focus between the two men as she cautiously backed away. They both erupted in laughter at her terror. Shear humiliation came over her as she bent down to pick up her shoes, before quickly exiting the courtyard. She could still hear them cackling hysterically as the door into the building closed behind her.

After entering, Lauren put on her shoes and scanned the room. She quickly spotted Cole and Cotton and made her way over to them. Lauren desperately needed to be as far away from this place as possible. During the attack, it seemed like time was in slow motion. Now, it was moving at a rapid pace.

Lauren demanded, "We are leaving right now!"

"You're such a buzz kill," said Cole. Lauren became angry. All she'd wanted to do was spend her evening in her trailer, talk to Davin, and go to sleep early. She never wanted to be out late on a Green Zone quest to collect her intoxicated roommates because they'd worn out their welcome. She certainly did not have a sexual assault on her agenda.

They were ungrateful, and Lauren was fed up. "I'm leaving," she said. "The Ambassador is not happy. If you don't come with me, he might call the Commander. It's up to you, but I'm leaving."

Lauren turned to walk away from them hoping they'd relent and return with her. She did not want to walk back alone. "Wait up," said Cotton. "Is he really mad?"

Lauren responded, "Can we go? I want to get out of here."

Lauren was relieved when they finally agreed to return to the trailer. After arriving, Cole and Cotton went straight to bed while Lauren locked herself in the bathroom to examine her body. She removed her shorts and underwear to find her privates covered in bright red, raw scratches. Her panties were also stained with blood. After shaking multiple loose pubic hairs into the toilet, she took her underwear and applied pressure to her vagina. Lauren placed her towel across the toilet seat cover and sat down to remove her t-shirt. Her head was pounding. She gently probed the back of it, and found a large goose egg. Lauren looked at her arms and legs. There would be a substantial amount of bruising as a souvenir. She hurt inside and out, but it all paled in comparison to the shame and degradation she felt. She was an armed soldier and could have pulled her weapon, but at what cost? Lauren stood to look at herself in the mirror. Uncontrollable tears were rolling down her cheeks. She couldn't face her reflection, so she closed her eyes and turned away. Lauren started the shower and once it was warm stepped in. After lathering her body in soap, she sat down in the corner of the shower stall and cried. She felt like a failure both emotionally and physically.

The next day Lauren dressed and reported for duty. She was thankful her uniform covered the marks left by her personal terrorist, Lieutenant Renzo. Lauren would still have to complete her assignment. She didn't know how to edit the footage into a story which would portray this man as anything other than the monster she secretly knew he was. Lauren sat and stared at her computer unable to concentrate most of the day. She stalled her editor when he asked about the story. Lauren hadn't told anyone what happened. From her experience with Sergeant First Class Edmundson, she was sure nothing would be done if she reported the assault. She was worried culpability would be directed at her given his position in a he said, she said standoff. Lauren was also concerned about making a statement regarding the incident. If she divulged the inebriated status of Cotton and Cole they would all get in trouble with their command; Cole and Cotton for violating General Order Number One and Lauren for not disclosing the event to the Major. "Nobody likes a rat," was a common saying in the military.

Lauren did not want this man to take her camaraderie. Then there was Davin. How would he react?

Lauren thought, *He might not ever want to touch me again.* What would telling him do anyway? Lauren knew he would be angry. He might even be angry at her. Lauren was lost in thought. This monster was so nice to her when she first met him. How could she have been so naïve? Why was the other man chanting 'Renzo Rhino?' Was it an ode to the Rhino Runner or a reference to violence or was it about sexual prowess? Lauren was glad he'd let her go, but also confused. Why had he released her? Several hours later, this man was still torturing her. Lauren was thankful when her day ended. She grabbed her editing laptop and headed back to her trailer. She'd have to finish putting something together there. Lauren hoped she would be able to concentrate a little better there too.

Chapter 8

Lauren was sitting outside her trailer editing a story together for the next day's Freedom Journal Iraq broadcast. She decided to scrap the Lieutenant Renzo and Italy's role within the Coalition piece entirely. Lauren had enough footage and interviews to go in another direction. She'd still do a feel-good piece, but instead, she'd make it about the Iraqi Security Forces. Lauren was in the midst of her story when Sergeant Chrisman stopped by her trailer. He was looking for Gray. It was apparent he'd developed a crush on her.

"Hey, is Specialist Gray around?" he asked. Lauren was the only one there.

She replied, "No. They all went to chow."

Chrisman inquired, "You didn't go?"

Lauren hadn't had an appetite all day. She told him, "I'm not hungry, and I have some work to finish. What are you up to?"

"I was going to ask Gray if she could talk to Peters. She always knows what to say," he said. "Anyway, Peters and his 'on again off again' girlfriend are off again. This girl is messing with his head. When I left this morning, he'd just talked to her and was upset. When I got back this evening, I found him in bed. It looks like he hasn't moved all day. He must have at some point because he wallpapered his side of the trailer in motivational quotes. I'm worried about him. I'm a guy. I don't know what to do. Maybe you could talk to him?"

Lauren was in the midst of her own emotional crisis. "I don't know if I'm the best person for the job," she said.

Chrisman pleaded, "Please. We'll just act like you're there for another reason. Do you need to borrow anything?" Lauren thought a moment. The wooden stoop she was sitting on was starting to hurt her already aching body.

She inquired, "Do you have one of those outdoor folding chairs?" Chrisman's face lit up.

"I sure do," he said.

Lauren agreed, "Alright, let me put this stuff inside."

Lauren returned her laptop to her room and followed Chrisman to his trailer.

Chrisman knocked on the door and said, "Heads up. Female incoming." He opened the door and they entered the room. Lauren looked around the tiny space. It was identical to hers except messier. Sergeant Peters was curled up in his bed beneath a mountain of covers. Chrisman had not exaggerated about the state Peters was in or the amount of paper hanging on the walls. Chrisman handed her the chair.

Lauren looked in Peters' direction and said, "Thanks for letting me borrow this. What's up with the burial mound over there?"

Peters shifted beneath the blankets and asked, "Is that Mayer?"

Chrisman answered, "Yeah. She's borrowing a chair." Peters uncovered his face and looked at her.

Lauren continued, "Are you okay? It looks like the inspiration fairy redecorated while you were checked out. I'm surprised there's no glitter."

Lauren looked over at Chrisman. He was smirking at her comment. Lauren had warned him. She didn't know what to say either. Peters sat up and threw off his covers.

"I'm about to go to chow," said Chrisman.

"You want to come, Mayer?" Lauren wasn't hungry, but she thought she should try to eat something.

"I guess. I haven't eaten yet," she replied.

Chrisman asked Peters, "You coming, dude?"

Peters nodded his head and silently put on his shoes while Lauren and Chrisman made small talk. When he was ready, they headed to the chow hall stopping on the way to leave the chair at her trailer.

When they arrived, Lauren wandered around looking at all the menu options. Nothing seemed appetizing. She eventually settled on a pear and a bottle of water before joining the two men at a table. The mountain of food on each of their trays versus her single pear was impressive.

Peters asked, "Is that all you're going to eat? You watching your figure or something?" They both started to laugh.

Lauren replied, "I'm not feeling well, so yes, this is all I'm going to eat."

Lauren changed the subject to the latest information coming through the broadcast operations office. It was a nice distraction from the bubblegum and duct tape editing she'd been doing to avoid dealing with her monster. When they were done eating, Lauren excused herself. She needed to get back to her trailer and finish her story.

Lauren called Davin that evening to talk. He was out again with his friends. He was having a lot of fun in Spain. Every letter he sent had some tidbit about his carefree adventures, and a lot of their phone calls involved him stepping out of a bar or venue to speak to her. Sometimes he would mention being hit on by women which inflamed Lauren's insecurities. It had started to wear on her. What began as envy was now resentment. Lauren knew he was beautiful. She knew Spain was beautiful. Lauren missed him so much and wanted to be with him, but she couldn't. When Davin mentioned how content he was she felt as though he didn't need her. After all, he was happy without her in paradise. As he once again, innocently, shared his latest escapades, Lauren became irritated. It wasn't his fault she had to be in Iraq or that a monster had attacked her. Lauren knew her anger was displaced, but she couldn't listen to how amazing things were for him or how much fun he was having. They were living in two different worlds, and hers wasn't nearly as pleasant. As Lauren began to spiral, Davin did all he could to connect with her. He sent her care packages and wrote more letters. It didn't matter though.

Lauren had started to distance herself emotionally. She was short with him when they spoke. She didn't know how to explain her rollercoaster of emotions, and she couldn't tell him what had happened. She couldn't tell anyone, and it was eating her up inside. Lauren began to think she should break up with Davin out of compassion but couldn't bring herself to do it. She eventually concluded it would be easier for them both if Davin left her. She could tell he was struggling to understand and navigate her contradictory moods. One minute, she loved him more than anything and the next she was actively pushing him away. It came as no surprise when one day after arguing Davin said, "Lauren I don't know what you want from me. I can't do this with you anymore. I can't handle it."

"I'm sorry you can't handle my deployment," she said crossly. "You have no idea what I'm going through."

In anger and haste, Lauren and Davin agreed to take a break from their relationship. While her halfhearted objective had been to push him away, Lauren was not prepared for the pain and loneliness she felt when he unknowingly complied. Lauren and Davin hardly spoke after that. They were both in pain. To cope, Lauren took up smoking. The cigarettes relieved her anxiety and suppressed her appetite which was helpful since she'd quit eating. It wasn't long before Lauren's healthy 5 foot 7 inch; 130-pound frame dwindled to 102 pounds. Cotton, Cole, and Gray were struggling too with their respective issues. Chasing stories all over Iraq for days, sometimes weeks at a time and homesickness were getting to them. Gray moved out after she and Cotton realized their personalities conflicted too much. Cotton and Cole took to blowing off steam together by going on outings to the palace pool or a local cafe. They'd invite Lauren, but she would decline. Instead, she opted to stay at the trailer alone after what had happened last time she was with them.

One evening as Lauren was sitting alone on her stoop in the dark, Sergeant Peters passed by. He backed up after spotting her lit cigarette.

"You smoke," he asked.

Lauren scoffed, "Yeah, lately."

Lauren's curiosity led her to ask, "What is it that you do around here?"

Peters continued, "Intelligence. I work the night shift. I get off in the morning. Maybe we could have breakfast sometime?"

Lauren made an excuse. "I never eat breakfast," she said.

Peter's replied, "You need to eat. You're looking thin, Mayer."

Lauren sarcastically replied, "Thanks?"

"I'm just saying eat something soon." Peters turned to walk away. After she was sure he was gone, Lauren lit another cigarette and smoked it before returning inside to observe herself in the bathroom mirror. She looked at her face. Lauren knew she was too thin. She wasn't sleeping well either. During the day, she barely had enough energy to move when she wore her heavy bulletproof vest or carried her weapon and camera equipment. Lauren regularly beat herself up for inflicting her stress on Davin the way she had. Nightly, she would lie awake in bed replaying their last conversation. Lauren wished she hadn't been mean to her best friend. She had lashed out at him because she was in pain. Most nights she would read his letters or stare at their photos which hung on the wall next to her bed. She would apologize to him repeatedly. Then she'd cry herself to sleep. Every morning when Lauren's alarm went off, she would force herself to get up and prepare for her day. As Lauren left the bathroom to find her bed, she knew this evening's routine would be the same. Tomorrow would be a new day, and she needed to attempt to get a little sleep.

The next morning, she awoke thinking the day's routine would be like any other. As she opened her front door and exited her trailer, she was caught by surprise. In the chair outside sat a single pear. Lauren stopped and picked it up. She wondered if Sergeant Peters had left it for her. Lauren passed his trailer every morning on her way to work. As she approached, she could hear a guitar. She found him sitting outside strumming a tune.

Lauren stopped and asked, "You just getting in?"

While he continued to play, Peters replied, "As a matter of fact, yes. You know, breakfast is the most important meal of the day."

He paused and smiled before continuing, "Did you get your pear?"

"Yes. Thank you," she responded.

Lauren pointed in the direction she needed to go and said, "I'm going to get to work now. Have a good day."

"You too," said Peters.

Lauren's routine changed after this. Every morning, she was not out on a mission, a pear would be waiting for her. Occasionally in the evenings, before he reported for duty, Peters would visit her and play his guitar while she sat outside editing or researching her next assignment. Sometimes her roommates would join them, and he would play for them all. Lauren liked watching him. He was surprisingly good, and the music was calming. As he played, Lauren thought about the day they'd first met. She was surprised how much her opinion of him had changed. He wasn't Davin. No one could ever replace Davin, but she was lonely, so she allowed his company.

Peters understood some of what she was experiencing. Both their relationships had cracked under the strain of separation and the emotional hardships that came with a deployment. He also knew what it was like to live in a place where evil men nurtured hate to cause death, destruction, and war. She and Peters often talked about their significant others or the situations they'd encountered while in Iraq. They were bonding and found comfort knowing they could relate to each other. One evening when he finished playing and stood to leave, Lauren informed him, "I'm headed out tomorrow. I'm doing a story on the Twenty-Third Iraqi Air Force Squadron."

"How long are you going to be gone," he asked.

Lauren continued, "I'm not sure."

Peters responded, "Well then. I'll play you one more song to tide you over until you get back. Any requests?"

Lauren laughed and said, "Not really."

"I know," he said. "This one's perfect."

Lauren, still seated on her stoop, looked up at him as he strummed the intro of the song.

Normally he just played, but for this one he began singing.

Lauren laughed and reminded him, "You're gonna be late for work."

With that, he backed away from her slowly while he continued to play and sing.

Lauren, still laughing, stood up and hollered as he disappeared around the corner, "You're a nut!"

Lauren headed out for her mission to Al-Muthana Air Base in Baghdad early the next day. When she arrived, she quickly located her point of contact. Her journey to her destination had gone smoother than expected and she was relieved. At the base, Coalition Forces were training the Twenty-Third Iraqi Air Force Squadron to re-establish Iraqi air support for policing international borders and transporting personnel, cargo, and equipment. Lauren observed and documented the airmen, C-130's, flight training, and maintenance operations. She flew all over Iraq with them throughout her week completing various missions. It had been an easy assignment, and her hosts were kind and hospitable. She was ready to get back though. She was always uneasy when she was alone meeting new people, especially men. Glad everything had gone well, Lauren said her goodbyes and began the objective of getting back to the Green Zone.

Sometimes it was harder to hitch a ride than others. Lauren often used her American Forces Network sway to get a seat on a Blackhawk helicopter when she wasn't on a flight manifest. She preferred the swiftness offered by this mode of transportation to the lengthy wait of the Rhino or danger of a convoy. After agreeing to record the flight for the pilots, Lauren was on her way home. When they arrived at the International Landing Zone, she handed one of the helicopter's crew members the tape she'd recorded. Lauren began to make her way back to her trailer. It was an exhausting two-mile walk in the intense heat. The weight of her equipment on her thin frame slowed her tremendously.

Eventually, she reached her trailer. Lauren was exhausted. With one last push, she made her way into her room and dropped all her gear on the floor with a thud. Lauren collapsed onto her bed. She was lying there catching her breath when she noticed light streaming through a hole above her head. Lauren sat up and looked around. In her pillow, she found a bullet that had come through her ceiling. Celebratory gunfire was a common practice among the Iraqis.

Lauren didn't understand why they did this so often. Inevitably, the rounds came back down. She sighed heavily as she held it in the palm of her hand. Now she'd have to go to the housing office and request a work order to repair it when all she wanted to do was rest. Lauren did just that. After reporting the incident and filling out the necessary paperwork, Lauren went back to her trailer.

She knocked on Cotton's door to let her know she was home. When Cotton answered, she said, "I'm home."

Cotton asked, "How was it?"

"It was good. I'm tired," said Lauren.

"Is Cole out?" Cotton confirmed Cole was gone on assignment. Lauren also asked if she'd gotten any mail while she was away.

"No mail that I know of," said Cotton. Lauren had sent Davin a letter before she left and was hoping maybe he'd sent something in return while she was gone. It had been weeks since they'd corresponded. Disheartened, Lauren showered and prepared for bed. She was in her nightgown when she heard a knock at the door. Lauren assumed it was a contractor coming to repair her ceiling. She put on her robe and answered the door, but was surprised to find Sergeant Peters.

"Your light was on so I thought I'd knock," he said.

"What are you up to?" she asked.

"I don't have to work tonight. My command gave me a few days off. I've missed hanging out with you on the stoop. I'm glad you're back. Do you want to hang out tonight?" he asked.

Lauren replied, "I'm very sleepy."

"I have movies," he said. "I was out on a foot patrol and bought a few bootleg DVD's from some kids. I'm sure there's something we can watch." Cole was gone. Even though Lauren was exhausted, she didn't want to sit alone feeling sorry for herself over Davin. She hesitantly agreed.

This pleased Peters. "Awesome! I'm going to go get the movies." He said, "I'll be right back," and exited the trailer.

Lauren left the door open so Peters could come in when he returned. She also wanted to avoid the perception of any impropriety should housing arrive. He'd never been in her trailer before.

"Everything is so girly and organized in here," he remarked as he stepped through her door with his DVDs in hand. Lauren laughed. Peters set the stack of movies next to the television.

As he looked around the room, he spotted Lauren's wall of Davin and inquired, "Are you with that guy or what?"

Lauren replied, "It's complicated. Besides, you have your whole girlfriend inspired motivational wallpaper thing going on in your trailer."

"True," he said, taking a backpack off and setting it on the floor.

"What's that for," she asked.

Peters shut her door and unzipped the backpack. He then pulled out a large bottle of rum.

"Why do you have that?" asked Lauren. Service members weren't supposed to drink, but there were a number of other entities operating in the Green Zone without this restriction.

"This is medicine," responded Peters.

"Medicine for what?" demanded Lauren. Peters pulled up his shirt to reveal his six-pack and chest. There was a large, ugly bruise in the center of his torso.

Lauren asked, "What happened?"

Peters sat down next to her on the bed and recounted, "I was on a foot patrol. We received some intelligence. Anyway, we ended up at a house where we performed a basic four-man stack for tactical entry and clearing. I was the first one in, and I took a round. My vest caught it, but the impact hurt."

"That foot patrol," Lauren asked as she pointed at the stack of DVD's.

"Well, I bought those before I got shot, but yes the same foot patrol," he said.

"That's why I have a few days off." Peters stood up and picked up the movies saying, "So, which one of these do you want to watch?"

Lauren responded, "I don't care."

Peters selected one off the top of the stack, put it in the DVD player, pushed play, and sat back down next to her on the bed. He poured himself a drink as the movie began.

He asked, "You want one?"

Lauren declined, "No, thank you." A few minutes in, Lauren realized the movie was a romantic comedy. As it progressed, it delved further and further into the complexities of love.

Lauren sneered, "This is dumb. Why are we watching this? They're all happy and it's making me sad. I'll take that drink now." Peters poured her a drink, and they continued to watch the movie.

It wasn't long before Lauren started to feel the effects of the alcohol and laid back on her bed saying, "I think I drank too much for what I weigh." At 102 pounds, she had almost no body fat. Peters, who was also tipsy, thought this was hilarious. They continued to joke, tease, and drink until the credits rolled. When the movie was over, he laid back next to her on the bed.

Lauren, reminisced, "Remember when you were saying those awful things about women and your girlfriend. Then later you were curled up in a ball dying because she ripped your heart out?"

Peters recalled, "Remember when your boyfriend said he couldn't handle your deployment. Then you cried and cried and quit eating, but you still kept everything he ever sent you plastered to your wall?"

Peters didn't know about her assault or that it had been the catalyst for her physical and mental deterioration. Now was not the time to explain how the majority of the conflict between her and Davin had been her fault.

"I know," she said. "Love is stupid. Feelings are stupid."

"Do you want to take it all down? I'll help you," he offered.

"No! Even if we're not together he's still my best friend," she said. Lying there, Lauren pointed out the hole in her ceiling.

"You like my new skylight," she asked.

Peters laughed and then turned his head to kiss her on the cheek. "You're my best friend here lately," he said.

Lauren had not been touched since the night she was violently assaulted. Despite being drunk and emotionally confused, Lauren knew she and Peters had become fond of each other. Lying next to him, Lauren felt desirable instead of dirty and disgusting. Peters kissed her again, and this time she kissed him back. A drunk Peters asked if he could sleep with her and an intoxicated Lauren consented. Initially, the intercourse was physically painful for Lauren, and emotionally she was overwhelmed by what was happening. She asked Peters to stop, and he complied. Instead, he held her until she asked him to leave. The whole interaction had been confusing, and Lauren needed time to herself to think about what she'd done.

The next day Cole returned. Lauren was glad she made it back safely. Cole told her all about her mission. Then they watched old episodes of the Maury Povich show.

As Cole made fun of the show's guests and their terrible predicaments, Lauren said, "I'd fit right in."

Cole asked, "What are you talking about?"

Lauren blurted out, "I kind of slept with Peters."

Cole responded in shock, "You did what?"

Lauren continued, "Please don't make me repeat it."

"Good for you," said Cole.

"I've heard you crying over Davin. Do you like Peters?"

Lauren was surprised by Cole's reaction. "I like him, but I love Davin," she replied.

"You need to get over Davin," Cole instructed. "A new guy is the best way to do that."

Lauren shared, "I'm confused right now. Also, I didn't let him finish. I was having some issues."

Cole advised, "Well if you're going to have sex with someone make sure you have an orgasm. There's no point in sleeping with anyone if you don't have an orgasm. You'll figure it out."

Lauren was flabbergasted by her advice. She wasn't sure what she had expected, but it certainly wasn't encouragement of this nature. Lauren didn't want to talk about it anymore, so she redirected Cole's attention to the show. Her life seemed to be getting more and more complicated. While it wasn't all her doing, her choices certainly weren't helping matters.

Lauren was juggling several complex issues at once. She was extremely confused about them all. However, her main concern was Davin. She still hadn't heard from him. She wanted to call, but the more time went on, the more awkward she felt about doing so. Lauren thought about him nonstop. She didn't want her pride to ruin her life, so she worked up the courage to phone him one evening.

He answered happily. "Hello, stranger," he said.

Lauren laughed and replied, "Hey. How are you?" She was so happy to hear the reassuring tone of his voice.

He continued, "I'm good. I've missed you. I'm sorry."

Lauren replied, "I'm sorry too. I've wanted to reach out to you, but I wasn't sure you'd want to hear from me. I wrote you instead, but I didn't hear back from you. I'm having a rough time. I don't know if it's okay to call you anymore. I apologize if it's not." Lauren wished she could curl up in his arms while they chatted.

"You haven't gotten my letters," he asked.

"No. I haven't," she said.

Davin assured her, "Lauren, I wrote you. I wrote you a couple of letters." This made Lauren feel better. At least she knew he hadn't completely forgotten about her.

"You can call me anytime," he said. "I don't want to lose you. I've been miserable."

Lauren understood the feeling and found a small bit of comfort in the knowledge he was miserable too. Lauren and Davin ended the conversation cordially. As she hung up, she was overcome with immense guilt over what she'd done with Peters. She wished she had called Davin sooner. Her stupid pride had gotten the best of her. Lauren didn't know what to do, but she did know she could never tell Davin. Her secrets were racking up quickly, and she was ashamed of every one of them.

Chapter 9

Lauren was feeling better after reconnecting with Davin. His packages and letters had also finally found their way to Iraq. Lauren felt stupid for thinking he'd abandoned her and ashamed for finding comfort in Sergeant Peters. The next days were uncomfortable. She didn't know where things were headed with Davin or if she should take Cole's advice and get over him with Peters. Davin held the potential for a beautiful future if they could survive the long distance, while Peters provided temporary comfort in her immediate unstable environment. Lauren tried to avoid Peters while she figured it out, but when he came around, she inevitably gave into his attention. She soon began emotionally juggling both men, and her conscience was a mess.

During this time, Lauren also became extremely insecure about Davin's female relationships. She'd question Davin's intentions when he spoke about his women friends. She attributed this to her own guilt. She felt terrible interrogating him when she had been guilty of the very thing she was accusing him of. It wasn't long before the repeated mention of his favorite female bartender was too much for Lauren to bear. After all, the men and women around her were almost all participating in some sort of physical or emotional affair. Even she had fallen into it. Lauren talked herself into believing Davin wasn't any different. He was alone in Spain and a sailor. Lauren knew all about their reputations.

Eventually, this insecurity and jealousy turned into an argument. Lauren was angry about many things. She'd never planned for her life to become this complicated. She felt like a crazy person hanging on with white knuckles to her morals and sanity. While Sergeant Peters was just another struggling human being in her proximity, he might as well have been Satan tempting her with the physical comfort and care she wanted and needed from Davin. Lost in a terrible mindset, Lauren sat outside her trailer brooding.

Her command had recently promoted her rank to Specialist. This was an accomplishment that should have brought her joy, but it didn't. She was angry at everyone and everything. Lauren didn't feel like the same person anymore, and she hated it. She was worried once Davin realized how much she'd changed he wouldn't want her anymore.

Lauren was contemplating completely severing ties with Davin. It was the kindest thing she could think of doing, but she didn't feel like she was mentally strong enough or capable of letting go of the love of her life. She thought about Cole's advice. She wasn't sure how replacing a human being with another could help her get over Davin, but Peters had inadvertently offered her just that. It wasn't long before Peters tempted her again and instead of declining, she gave in. Their second intimate encounter was less awkward than the first.

Afterward, they talked about what it meant. "Are you going to start calling me John now?"

Lauren replied sarcastically, "Sure thing, John."

"What made you change your mind?" he asked.

Lauren hesitantly said, "I'm trying something new?"

"I wish you hadn't of waited so long," he responded.

Lying on his side in her bed, he kissed her shoulder. "My company is leaving in a couple of weeks," he informed her.

Lauren didn't know this, and she didn't know how she should feel about it.

They were laying in silence when he suddenly asked, "Can you take his stuff down now?" Lauren looked up at her walls and over to her nightstand. Davin was everywhere. She wasn't prepared for her reaction to this request. She wasn't even sure why the question had irritated her. It wouldn't have been an unreasonable request under normal circumstances, but nothing about her life was normal anymore.

Lauren sat up and put on her clothes.

"What's wrong?" John asked.

"I'm not ready to take him down. You don't get to ask me to do that. I'll put him away when I want to," she said.

John apologized, "I'm sorry. It just makes me uncomfortable, Lauren." He sat up, wrapped his arms around her waist, and pulled her close. "Come here. You do whatever you need to do. I understand," he said.

Lauren demanded, "Don't talk about him. I don't know what I'm doing or what this is. You just said you were leaving. You don't get to talk about him."

He agreed, "You're right." Lauren eased her defensive posture. Her mind was reeling in confusion and chaos. Lauren felt like an emotional mess and wanted Peters to leave.

"Please go," she said. "Please. I just want to be alone now." Peters stood and dressed in compliance. Before he left, he wiped a tear from her cheek and kissed her goodbye.

The next day Lauren left on another mission. She was glad to have the distraction and set out to document the women of Operation Iraqi Freedom. She spent two weeks jumping from one forward operating base to another. When she finally found her way home, she was exhausted. The women she interviewed seemed strong and resilient. Lauren seemed that way, too, by outward appearance. She wondered if they were struggling under their own facades. While resting in bed, Lauren looked at photos from her assignment. She glanced over to her nightstand at the photograph of Davin. His charming smile and kind gaze were fixed in time. She wished she were somewhere with him looking at his beautiful face and listening to his magnetic musings in person. Her thoughts then turned to John. She wasn't sure if he was still in the International Zone or not. Lauren would miss him, but she was glad he was going home. John had been there for a while and deserved to be back with his loved ones. Lauren thought about how upset they'd both been over their significant others and hoped he would work things out with his.

Later that day, Lauren heard a knock at her door and answered it. It was John. "I missed you," he said. "I was afraid you wouldn't get back before I left." Lauren had secretly hoped she would miss his departure.

She was confused about their relationship. "I'm here," she said.

John continued, "We're leaving sometime tomorrow."

Lauren felt sadness creep over her. After he was gone, she'd have no one to talk too. John had willingly filled a void. He'd become her friend and then some. Lauren knew she shouldn't, but since she might never see him again, she kissed him. He kissed her back passionately. Before she knew it, they were in her bed again. *Dammit,* Lauren thought. She didn't know what was wrong with her. She was completely distracted by her inner dialog of reprimand during intercourse. She had no idea why she was even allowing the current situation to take place. As John climaxed, Lauren was pulled back to attention by the words, "I love you."

She wondered if she had heard what she thought she had. When John finished, Lauren pushed him off of her and sat up.

"You love me?"

John was puzzled, "What?"

"You just said 'I love you'," she said.

"I did?" he questioned. "I guess I do."

"John you're leaving," she replied. "You're going home. I know you're going to reconnect with your girlfriend."

John nodded in affirmation. "I'll miss you," he said.

Lauren understood how he felt. She'd miss him too. She'd grown to care about him very much but knew she couldn't offer more even if she earnestly tried. Lauren was completely and hopelessly tangled in Davin.

Placing a hand on his chest, Lauren requested, "Promise you'll keep in touch."

John took her hand and kissed the top of it. "I promise," he said.

After John left, Lauren had a hard time adjusting to his absence. She had not realized how much she'd miss him or how much she'd taken his kind gestures for granted. There were no more pears in the morning; No more relaxing guitar sessions in the evening. John kept his promise though. They emailed back and forth updating each other periodically. Lauren wrote that she missed him. She wrote about her assignments and life in the Green Zone. He understood the war zone and the soldier part of her world.

As John reintegrated into his environment, he and Lauren corresponded less and less until their exchanges tapered off. Lauren kept his emails though. She'd re-read them from time to time. He seemed happy, and Lauren was glad he'd been able to work things out with his significant other. Their time together had been brief and surreal given the circumstances. Nonetheless, Lauren was still in love with Davin. She wanted to work things out with him the way John had with his girlfriend. Lauren wrote to Davin as often as possible. She wrote him about how much she loved him and how she wished she were with him. Davin loved the carefree girl she still wanted to be; the one before she became this damaged, twisty, unrecognizable version. She missed him immensely and decided to give him a call.

He answered his phone almost immediately. "Hey," she said when she heard the line pick up.

"Follow me for a second. There's so much going on around here."

After listening to her updates, he asked, "Lauren, are you okay?"

"Yes," she replied. Lauren's rotation for rest and recuperation was coming up. Soldiers who were serving in areas designated as hostile fire and imminent danger areas were eligible to leave for a two-week reprieve. "I can't wait to get out of here," she vented.

"This place is crazy. I'm scared. I'm going crazy too. I've started my countdown for R&R."

"Really?" he asked.

"When are you getting to leave?"

"Sometime right after the New Year," she responded. "I'd like to see you."

"I want to see you too," he said. Lauren's heart was immensely comforted by his admission.

She smiled. "Alright, I'll let you know once I have more details. I'm excited. I finally have something to look forward too."

The next few weeks Lauren spoke with Davin as often as she could. She made it through the holidays without too much homesickness. Knowing she would soon be reunited with her family and best friend made it all bearable. Finally, the day arrived for her journey home.

As Lauren began her trip, she was nervous. It had been seven months since she'd seen Davin. A lot had happened in that time. She knew she should tell Davin everything, but decided she didn't want to ruin the two-week break she had from her reality. It was a selfish decision, but she'd been surrounded by plenty of pain and hate. She couldn't help but want to avoid experiencing or causing more. When she arrived at the airport to Davin's waiting arms, a sensation of home washed over her. All the bad things she'd been troubled by suddenly didn't exist in his embrace. He truly was her soul mate and her heart's abode. If he ever knew her secrets, it would devastate him beyond repair. Lauren couldn't bear the thought and hated herself for becoming such a potentially destructive human being. She could never tell him. She'd lose him, and she needed him so much. Lauren shoved it all into a black hole in her mind and pretended none of it existed. Keeping their usual routine, Davin whisked her away to their hotel room where they quickly reacquainted themselves intimately.

Afterward, they laid together naked, affectionately spooning, enjoying each other's intoxicating aroma, and talking about their future. "I wish we could stay this way forever," Lauren said.

Davin kissed her, "I know. Me too. I love you so much, Lauren."

Lauren replied, "I love you too. I hate that place. I wish I didn't have to go back. There's so much bad. I need something to remind me of good." Davin kissed the back of her neck and held her tight in his warm embrace. Lauren wanted to belong to him more than ever.

She asked, "Would you still want to marry someone like me?" Lauren knew what she meant even if he didn't.

"Of course, I would," he said.

"I want to marry you too someday," she said.

After a moment of silence, Davin offered, "Then let's get engaged."

"You need something to remind you of good. Our love is just that."

Lauren turned to face him. "Do I get a ring?" she asked.

Davin confirmed, "Yes. A beautiful ring for my beautiful soldier."

Lauren's heart was pounding with excitement. "Really?" she asked skeptically.

"Let's shower and go shopping," he said. "We're going to get you something amazing." Davin got up out of bed.

Lauren's eyes followed him as his entered the bathroom. "Come on," he yelled as he turned on the water. "What are you waiting for?"

After finding the nearest mall and visiting several jewelry stores, Lauren found a ring she could not live without. It was stunning, white gold, and vintage inspired. The engagement ring possessed a dazzling two-karat princess cut diamond. It was also flanked by two additional half karat cut diamonds, and encrusted with thirty twinkling accent stones. Lauren was smitten.

As she placed it on her finger, she commented, "Davin, it's beautiful."

Davin replied, "It is. I guess we need the matching band too?"

Lauren hadn't thought about it. "Really?" she asked.

Davin replied, "You'll need a wedding band when we get married, right?"

Lauren kissed him enthusiastically. He could do no wrong. She knew him well, but somehow, he always managed to surprise her. Davin was a thoughtful and kind man. He was everything she ever wanted. Davin asked for the wedding band as well. The band featured thirty-nine alluring round cut diamonds and intricate detailing. On Lauren's delicate hand, the pair looked like icing.

As he finalized the purchase, he watched her admire her hand, "You take my breath away, Lauren." Lauren kissed him again, and they happily left the store to arrange a dinner so their families could finally meet.

At dinner, Davin announced their engagement. Everyone was happy and excited for the two. Lauren and Davin were over the moon at how well their families got along. As Lauren sat and watched the parties acquaint themselves, she thought about how Davin had made the time they had together the best she could imagine. Lauren would have to return to Baghdad in the coming days, but she'd be taking a beautiful reminder of their love with her. Eight more months of separation were ahead of them. She knew it would be tough, but she had every intention of coming home to marry this man. Davin caught her gazing at him and smiled. Lauren mouthed I love you. He mouthed back; I love you too.

The day arrived for Lauren to return to Iraq. She sat in silence most of the drive to the airport. She, her mother, father, and Davin were all quiet. Returning to a war zone was a difficult and lengthy task, but one she had to do. Lauren was having a hard time keeping it together. Returning to the Green Zone was the last thing she wanted to do. It was her duty though, so she tried to muster as much motivation and optimism as she could for herself and her loved ones. These goodbyes were hard for her, but they were much worse for the people she was leaving behind. She'd already spent several months there and knew what she'd be going back too. For her family and Davin, it was unfamiliar territory. Lauren understood and did her best to minimize their fears with reassurances when she felt like they were needed.

When they arrived at the airport, Lauren checked in and located the USO lounge to check in with them as well. There she found other service members awaiting the same fate.

Lauren turned to her family and said, "I'll be fine. I love you all." She hugged each member of her sending party and stayed with them as long as she could. It wasn't long though. Within minutes a military liaison arrived to escort the waiting soldiers to their flight. As she said her final goodbyes, she tried to keep it together. Her mother's weeping didn't faze her, but when she looked into Davin's tear-filled eyes, she couldn't help herself any longer. It took every bit of strength and motivation she had to turn and walk away. Lauren joined the rest of the group and began to walk toward their gate. After boarding, she found her seat and fought back her tears. She didn't want to cry in front of her fellow soldiers. They were all having a rough morning and bawling about it wasn't going to garner sympathy, improve the situation, or provide any comfort. The last thing she needed was a snotty nose or a headache.

It took almost seventy-two hours to make her way back. She'd been able to secure a seat on one of the Rhino's early morning runs to the Green Zone. The sunrise was still hours away. As Lauren walked through the compound toward her trailer, she was struck by the smell. It always smelled terrible from the trash burning in open burn pits or raw sewage wafting from some location. It was just another thing, like the dust storms, or the sounds of helicopter rotors, mortars, and celebratory fire, she'd come to get used to and accept. When she arrived at her trailer, she entered as quietly as possible. She wasn't sure if Cole was home, but she didn't want to wake her if she was. In the tiny living quarters, it was impossible not to disrupt a sleeping roommate.

Cole called out, "Mayer. Is that you?"

Lauren answered, "Yes. Sorry. I'll get settled in a minute."

Cole responded, "No, it's okay. You can turn on the light." Lauren had missed her trailer mates. They'd become close and leaned on each other for support quite often.

"Thank you," Lauren said. Lauren quickly deposited her things and changed her clothes. She'd been wearing the same uniform for days. It desperately needed to be washed. She also needed a shower. Cole gave her the main points and caught her up on the things she'd missed while she was away. It was the usual command drama. Afterward, Lauren excused herself to shower. She could get a couple of hours of sleep before reporting back to work if she hurried and got to bed. By the time she found her mattress, she could barely keep her eyes open. She hadn't realized how exhausted she was until she was able to slow down. Lauren fell asleep almost immediately. It was a welcome accomplishment.

When Lauren arrived at work, she reported to her Major for check-in. While visiting, the Major informed her she'd been switched to the special projects department. Special projects entailed meeting with congressional delegates and any other duties that did not fit into the news production or radio station elements of their mission. Lauren was thrilled. She would no longer have to go on solo missions, chase down leads, or have to document stories from the "front lines of the war on terror", as their newscast put it. She was relieved.

After her encounter with Lieutenant Renzo, she had developed an intense aversion to traveling alone to meet strangers in unfamiliar locations. She would still have to travel periodically. However, most of special project's missions required two people so she would not be alone. Lauren was switched because she was good at her job, but also because she was one of the few soldiers in her detachment that had a passport and had brought it along with her. Lauren didn't care she'd gotten the new assignment mostly by default. Learning her first mission would be a trip to Turkey with the Iraqi Air Force, and a group of children made it a win regardless of the reasons in which she'd obtained it. Lauren found her news editing workspace and packed her things to relocate to her new office. Sergeant First Class Matt Simmons was the head of the special projects department.

He greeted her happily, "Hello there, Specialist Mayer. Welcome to your new digs!"

Lauren was fond of Sergeant First Class Simmons. He was witty, and known to step in on behalf of the female soldiers when he saw or heard Sergeant First Class Edmundson being inappropriate.

"Hi. I heard we're going somewhere," she said.

Sergeant First Class Simmons was excited, "Yes, we are! Turkey! Can you believe it?"

Lauren could not. "Yeah, what's up with that?"

Chapter 10

Lauren spent her remaining months in Iraq surprisingly stress-free. She and Davin's relationship was back on track. They'd had the occasional tiff, but were stronger than ever. Lauren's time in special projects was also ticking along seamlessly, and soon the countdown to the arrival of the detachment's replacements began. Everyone seemed energized and ready for departure. It wasn't long before the official handoff of duties came and went. After weeks of preparing and packing, Lauren's group was headed home.

First, they'd have to stop in Kuwait to process out of the country. Lauren had not been able to speak to Davin before their departure. Communication when traveling in and out of Iraq was discouraged due to operational security concerns. Upon landing in Kuwait, the Commander gave the green light to phone loved ones. Lauren and a group of soldiers from her command made their way to the communications tent to call home. She decided to dial Davin first.

The phone rang, and Davin answered abruptly, "Hello." His tone was not pleasant. He did not seem as thrilled as Lauren thought he'd be after not hearing from her for days.

"Davin, we made it to Kuwait," she said. "Is everything okay?"

"No," replied Davin. Lauren was lost.

"What's wrong?" she asked.

Davin angrily replied, "I know about you and John. How could you?" He began to cry. Lauren's heart was suddenly in her throat. She racked her brain. How could he have possibly found out?

"What do you mean?" she asked.

"I didn't hear from you for days, so I decided to check your email. I found and read all the emails exchanged between the two of you," he reported.

Lauren was furious. He knew she was not able to talk at times due to communication blackouts. He was a sailor for heaven's sake and subject to the same orders from time to time.

"You hacked into my email," she asked crossly. Lauren felt completely violated. She imagined he was feeling something similar. "Why would you do that?" she asked.

"Why would you?" he replied.

Lauren felt ashamed. She hadn't seen Sergeant John Peters since the day he left Iraq, and their communications had stopped before her visit with Davin on R&R. It was August now. Many months had passed. To Lauren, it felt like her time with Peters had ceased a lifetime ago, but to Davin, it was brand new. Lauren didn't know what to say. Things with Davin had been very rocky for a bit. She wasn't even sure what the nature of her relationship with Davin was during her moment of desperate confusion. She now knew it had all been a colossal mistake. Lauren was finally going home to begin the next chapter of her life with him, and it was all going to end before it even started. He'd put her on the spot. Lauren didn't know how to tell Davin about her assault. She didn't know how to explain Peters. She had hoped it would all disappear like the dust on her boots once she was home.

Lauren didn't know what to say next. She blurted out, "I was assaulted."

"By John?" he asked. "Did he rape you?"

Lauren suddenly remembered where she was. She responded, "I have to go. Other people are waiting for the phone. I love you. I'm sorry."

Lauren hung up the phone and waited in a corner for Cole to wrap up her conversation. On their way back to their temporary quarters, Lauren told Cole, "Davin knows about Peters."

Cole was shocked and asked, "How?" Lauren told her about the phone conversation leaving out the portion about the assault.

"Damn," said Cole.

"Is he going to be in Texas when we get back?"

"He was," said Lauren.

"I don't know if he'll be there now."

"Don't let him get to you,"

Cole continued. "You cried almost every night over him for a while. It was hard to watch. He wasn't there. We all did some messed up stuff there. We all survived. We're all going home."

Repeating this to herself the rest of the long, tiring journey made her feel a little better. It wasn't much of a reprieve though. She knew she'd handled the whole situation poorly and was disappointed in herself. Her parents had raised her better. No amount of rationalizing could clear her conscience. Lauren knew she'd have to explain everything to Davin if she ever spoke to or saw him again. She couldn't bear the thought of him knowing every detail of their time apart. She was not ready to deal with the assault or her actions in its aftermath.

From Kuwait, the group traveled to Fort Dix, New Jersey and then on to Texas. They arrived at Fort Hood. The heat index exceeded the triple-digit mark, but it felt nice compared to the heat of the desert. Lauren's unit would have to stay on base and demobilize. During demobilization, the military would remove the unit's status from active service back to reserve capacity. The process took about a week. Lauren found herself experiencing a mix of confusing emotions. She was happy and relieved to know she'd soon be home with her family. She also found herself feeling anxious and immensely depressed.

Lauren and Davin had only exchanged brief words since the last revealing conversation in Kuwait. She was nervous, as she should have been, to know what would happen with their relationship. Through limited communication, they agreed to hash it all out in person when he arrived from Spain. Lauren was hopeful everything would be alright after Davin confirmed he would not cancel his return to the states. Their week at Fort Hood finally drew to a close, and the Commander dismissed the unit. Lauren was received by the welcoming arms of her family. It felt nice to be home. This crazy chapter of her life was almost closed. She'd have to wait for Davin to arrive to finish it for good.

Lauren nervously waited at baggage claim. She wished she had the wine she'd left at the hotel in hand as she paced back and forth. It seemed like an eternity of waiting. She rehearsed what she should say to Davin under her breath as she periodically checked the information boards for flight updates. None of her words seemed sufficient. She wondered if she should hug him or not. Lauren was preparing herself for an awkward reception when she finally spotted him walking toward her. She stood frozen in an insecure manner. Lauren didn't know what to do. He was her beautiful soul mate, and she had wounded him brutally. She felt terrible but was also upset by his violation of her privacy. Lauren could see the sorrow in his eyes as he approached her. This reunion was very different from the ones before. This one was bittersweet and uncomfortable. It didn't stop him from embracing her though. Davin hugged her tight. Surprised, Lauren hugged him back. After a moment, she kissed his cheek and took his hand. Together, they silently left the airport and headed to their hotel to have a conversation they'd both been dreading.

When Lauren and Davin arrived at their hotel room, they made small talk. Lauren wanted to make love to him. She wanted to hold him tight, but instead sat down on the bed and asked, "How was your flight?"

Davin recounted a few details in a detached manner before telling her, "I'd like to take a shower."

"Okay," Lauren replied.

Davin left Lauren and entered the bathroom. Lauren listened for the shower to begin before retrieving a corkscrew from her suitcase. She pulled the cork and swilled straight from the bottle of wine. As Davin showered, Lauren sat nervously on the bed anticipating what would happen next. Finally, the water turned off, and Davin stepped back into the room. He began to towel off in front of her. His physique was beautiful. Lauren sighed heavily before directing her gaze to the floor.

"I'm sorry," she said. Davin wrapped the towel around his waist.

"I emailed John. He said he didn't take advantage of you," Davin reported.

Lauren was irritated, "You emailed him?" Davin nodded his head in affirmation.

Lauren replied, "A lot was going on. I was confused and heartbroken about our relationship. It happened. It was almost a year ago now."

Davin accused her, "You lied, and it hasn't been a year for me. I just found out!" Lauren had not lied, but she had not clarified either. Secretly, Lauren preferred he believe she was a liar rather than re-live the horrible details of her assault. While John had not been her assailant, she had been attacked. Davin probably wouldn't believe her now anyway if she did tell him the truth about the assault and her subsequent relationship with Peters.

She apologized again. "I'm truly sorry." In silence, Davin sat down on the bed next to her. Lauren leaned her head over and placed it on his shoulder.

She whispered, "I love you."

Davin leaned his head against the top of hers and replied, "I love you too." They were both a mess of emotions. Lauren kissed Davin's skin. He returned the gesture with a kiss on her crown. After a moment, Lauren reached her lips to his neck and kissed him again before pulling away to look him in the eyes. Davin gazed at her a moment before kissing her mouth tenderly.

In an attempt to restore their intimacy, Lauren kissed her lover back passionately. The mixture of brokenhearted grief and desperate desire to reclaim each other sexually was mutual. Lauren and Davin were both scared. Against better judgment, they continued to kiss and caress each other lovingly. It wasn't long before Davin could not endure a second more without penetrating her. Lauren ached for her soul mate too. She stopped him as he pulled her clothes off piece by piece.

"Are you sure?" she asked. Davin laid her back on the bed. He gently spread her legs, climbed on top of her, and thrust his penis into her wet vagina. Lauren let out a gasp of pleasure as he entered her. He continued to rhythmically push himself deeper and deeper. Their lovemaking was more passionate than it had ever been before. They spent the remainder of Davin's week-long visit similarly intertwined. Each encounter was even more intense than the last. It wasn't all sex though. Lauren and Davin did occasionally leave their room to wander in the light of day and discuss their future as a couple. They both still loved each other immensely, and neither could imagine a life without the other in it.

One day while roaming around a quaint town square, Davin proposed they visit the courthouse positioned in its center and get married. "Let's get married. We're both in the military so we wouldn't have to wait," he said.

Lauren was caught off-guard. "What?" she asked.

"We could do it today," he said. Lauren thought about it for a moment. She and Davin had been planning a traditional wedding for their loved ones.

After the uncertainty they'd faced in their relationship, both agreed to halt all wedding plans. Lauren was nervous about Davin's suggestion. They loved each other very much, but how could their mess suddenly be daisies after a brief reconciliation?

"I don't know, Davin," she said. Lauren did not want to make any more mistakes.

Davin continued, "You need someone to take care of you, Lauren. I will take care of you. I promise to love you. If we get married now, you can come back with me to Spain. We'll work on us some more and decide where we go from there. Let's get married."

Lauren was terrified her emotions were clouding her decision-making skills, but she desperately wanted to be his wife. She agreed, "Ok. Let's do it."

Davin and Lauren entered the County Clerk's office and purchased a marriage license. They were able to secure an appointment with the Justice of the Peace within minutes. The recital of vows was standard. Wearing nothing special, they earnestly made commitments to each other wholeheartedly. When all was said and done, they were man and wife. In all, the process took no more than an hour. Now, Lauren had a new name. She was officially Mrs. Davin Hendrix. When Lauren and Davin told their families they had eloped, all were surprised. Lauren had found herself homeless upon returning from her deployment to Texas and everything she owned was still packed away in storage. She had no military obligations to attend to in her immediate future due to a six-month post-deployment duty reprieve. Marrying Davin and moving to Spain with him seemed as good a plan as any. Davin purchased her a ticket on his flight. When the day came for him to return to Rota, Spain, they both boarded hand in hand to begin their life as a married couple.

Upon arriving in Spain, they retrieved their bags from baggage claim, found his car, and headed toward what would be her new home. Lauren reminisced as they drove through the countryside about her last visit. She'd changed so much since then. Davin would have to get to know a relatively new person. Lauren was grappling with her demons while reintegrating into a civilian world. She looked the same on the outside, but a lot had changed inside. Lauren wasn't sure he'd even stopped to fully evaluate the changes in her personality. Davin was also slowly adjusting to marriage while struggling with trust issues due to her indiscretion. He'd promised to love and take care of her though. He'd talked her into a Justice of the Peace marriage. All Lauren could do was hope for the best.

As the weeks turned to months, Lauren and Davin found themselves trying to maneuver through married life. There were times when they fought intensely, but they always made up passionately in bed before falling asleep. Their love and devotion to each other were consistent throughout it all. Lauren knew most of their issues stemmed from her actions during their time apart. She held her tongue as much as possible during arguments. She knew he loved her no matter what was said. It did take a toll, however. Lauren found herself sinking deeper and deeper into depression. She was dealing with an overwhelming amount of anxiety as well. Lula, his rescue puppy, provided most of Lauren's entertainment. She was glad to have a comforting companion but hated walking her alone during the day. Lauren found herself rarely leaving the apartment without Davin. The only time she felt safe was when she was with him. It made for a monotonous life. No matter how many pep talks she gave herself, Lauren couldn't shake her feelings of uneasiness. Her monster, Lieutenant Renzo, still actively invaded her thoughts. Her secret was eating her up inside. He was affecting her relationship with Davin. He was influencing her day to day routine. He was manipulating her sanity. Lauren mentally fought him off every day, and it was taking a secret toll.

One day, Davin returned home from work extremely excited.

"Guess what," he posed. Lauren was washing dishes.

She stopped and dried her hands. "Guess," he insisted. She furrowed her brow in amusement as she turned toward him, crossed her arms, and leaned against the kitchen sink. Davin was ecstatic and giddy.

"Ummmm, I don't know," laughed Lauren.

"No guesses?" He continued, "I have new orders. Drum roll please!" He proceeded to drum on the kitchen table. Lauren was hoping it would be orders back to the states. She loved Spain but truly wanted to be closer to Texas.

"Where?" she asked eagerly.

Davin enthusiastically announced, "We are going to Naples, Italy!" His words instantly transformed her unaware blissful amusement to feelings of intense terror. Davin's voice and the grin on his face were priceless.

Lauren feigned excitement, "Naples, Italy? Really? Is that where you wanted to go?" Lauren's mind was racing. Her monster was from the NATO base in Naples, Italy. She felt like she could hardly breathe as her anxiety shot through the roof.

"When did you ask to be transferred to Italy?" she asked.

Davin proudly recounted, "Well, as you know, my orders here are about to expire. I've been watching the assignment slots. Italy popped up, and I submitted for it as soon as I saw it! This opportunity will be amazing for us!"

Lauren was outwardly calm, but her thoughts were troubled. He hadn't even mentioned Italy to her. All their talks about his next assignment had involved locations in the states. Lauren wasn't sure what to say next. Davin didn't know about Lieutenant Renzo. At this point, Lauren still wasn't ready to share her monster with him. She loved him. He was her husband. She'd have to go to Italy if she wanted to be with him. It was done, and he had the orders. In no time at all, they'd be moving to Naples. They'd be at a base in proximity to the NATO base and a person she'd hoped she would never see again.

Lauren took a deep breath, "That does sound amazing. Wow, we're going to be Italians."

To distract him from any unease in her voice, Lauren uncrossed her arms and joked, "I guess I should start using my hands more when I talk." Lauren waved her arms around wildly as she said this. Davin burst into laughter. He then walked over and wrapped his arms around her waist.

Now standing face to face, he said, "I'm so glad you're my wife. I know you wanted to be closer to your family, but this really is a great opportunity for my career. I thought about you too. You can work at the American Forces Network - Naples for your reserve duties. We're going to have a lot of fun."

Lauren kissed him, "Aye, aye, Captain." Davin had always been more adventurous than she. Lauren knew this.

Davin released his arms from her waist, "So, what's for dinner?"

Lauren replied, "I guess I should make something Italian."

Davin kissed each of her cheeks in European form and said, "Grazie, Bella."

Lauren laughed, "Go change your clothes!" Davin exited the kitchen to change out of his uniform. At that moment, she wished she'd been honest from the beginning. The more time passed, the harder it was to tell him. Lauren closed her eyes and whispered a prayer, "Dear God. Please give me strength." With that, Lauren pulled her ingredients and began preparing a celebratory Italian inspired meal.

Chapter 11

Their last few weeks in Spain went quickly. Davin and Lauren agreed she would return to the states to report to her unit. She'd need to submit a request to perform her reserve duties at the American Forces Network in Naples. During her time at AFN - Iraq, Lauren had served with a Navy Senior Chief who was stationed at AFN - Naples. Upon receiving the duty request, Senior Chief Petty Officer Adam Lucus was delighted to approve her application. Lauren's command proceeded to make the appropriate arrangements. Meanwhile, Davin, Lula, and their household belongings were making their transfer from Spain to Italy.

Once Davin arrived safely and set up housing, Lauren would meet him there. Lauren was excited to see her husband again, but she was also dreading what was ahead of her. Her monster consumed her thoughts. What if she ran into him? What would she say? How would she react? What would he do? What if Davin was there when it happened? Lauren occupied her time at home with her family as much as possible. Davin kept her updated with his progress as he went along.

Finally, the day came when he was ready for her to join him. Lauren packed her bags, said goodbye to her family, and boarded a plane destined for Naples. She'd taken many long, uncomfortable flights but none compared to the difficulty she was having aboard this one. Her only consolation was that Davin would be waiting for her with his beautiful smile and comforting embrace when she landed.

Lauren arrived in Naples on a February Day. It was Valentine's Day, and Davin was waiting for her at the airport like always. As she approached him in baggage claim, she could see he had a small white box in hand and a bouquet of calla lilies. Lauren liked roses, but Davin knew calla lilies were her favorite. Lauren couldn't help but adore this man. He was always thoughtful. "What's all this," she asked. Davin handed her the flowers and opened the box to reveal a beautiful three stone diamond necklace.

"Lauren, I just want to show you how much I appreciate you. I know you wanted to be closer to your family. You've been very supportive, and I love you."

Lauren started to cry. It was as if he knew all about her mental struggle and despair over her monster. While they waited for her suitcase to arrive, Davin placed the necklace on her neck. Lauren relished his sweet gesture. When he was done fastening the clasp, he stepped back and examined her. "You are beautiful, Lauren." With flowers in hand, Lauren threw her arms around his neck and embraced him tightly.

Weeping into his shoulder, she said, "Sorry. I'm getting snot on you."

Davin chuckled, "You hate snot!"

She laughed and exclaimed, "I know!"

When Lauren's bag arrived, Davin collected it and together they made their way to their temporary quarters. Davin had selected a home for them to live in off-post. However, it would not be ready to move into until the following day. Lauren was uneasy about living off-post but knew it was what Davin wanted. He loved immersing himself in the culture of whatever country in which the Navy placed him. She loved that about him, and it didn't matter to her where they lived as long as they were together.

The next day, while they explored the base, Davin received a call. It was the housing office.

Davin cupped the receiving end of his cell phone and whispered, "Lauren, we can go pick up the keys." Lauren smiled as she listened. All the newness, excitement, and Davin's affection had created a welcome distraction from the monster weighing on her mind. Davin thanked the other party and hung up.

"Do you want to go set up delivery of our property and get the key?"

Lauren retorted, "What kind of a question is that? Of course, I do."

Davin proceeded to brag, "I did well. The house is gorgeous, and the landlord is fantastic. You're going to love it!"

Davin and Lauren headed toward the car. They drove over to the housing office to schedule the delivery of their property for the following day, and to pick up their keys before heading off base. The house was located in a small community named Casapesena. As they drove through the quaint town, Lauren fell in love. "This is charming."

Davin smiled and said, "I knew you'd like it." A picturesque coffee shop next to a beautiful courtyard caught Lauren's eye. Several little old men sat out in the sunshine bantering happily.

"Davin look. They're adorable." Davin smirked as though he were thoroughly pleased with her delight.

"Wait until you see the house," he said as he slowed the vehicle and pulled around a corner. There on a dead-end street, behind a gate, stood a beautiful two-story Mediterranean style home. Davin punched in a code, and the gate opened.

"This is our house? We're going to live here?" she asked in disbelief. Davin pulled through and parked in the driveway.

He turned off the car and looked over at her, "Lauren, I know you need to feel safe. I need to know you're safe too. I'll be on a ship a lot while we're here. The landlord is very friendly. If anything, ever happens, you can call her. She assured me she'd be available. She lives down the street."

Lauren appreciated his concern and replied, "Thank you." She exited the car and stood in the driveway taking it all in. Across the street, Lauren could see a small Catholic church surrounded by a field of bright red poppies. Davin got out of the car and made his way over to her.

"What do you think?" he asked.

Lauren kissed him and answered, "I think I want to see what's inside." Davin handed her the key, and she was off. Lauren couldn't believe how beautiful the house was. She made her way up the stone walk and across a large wrap around porch to the front door. Lauren opened it to find a high-ceilinged marble palace with a grand staircase. She turned back to look at Davin who had just caught up.

"We can afford to live here?" she asked.

Davin replied, "Yes, the Navy is going to pay for us to live here."

Lauren was still in shock. "Come on. I'll give you the tour," he said. Inside, Davin introduced Lauren to an ample family room, lovely kitchen, two bathrooms, and three spacious bedrooms, each with its own balcony. It was three times the size of the apartment they'd lived in when they were in Spain. From the window in the upstairs bathroom, Lauren could see a grape vineyard just over the back wall.

She yelled to Davin who was downstairs, "Davin, there's wine in the backyard!" Lauren could hear his laughter as it echoed off the marble of the empty space. She headed back down to find him.

"How much are you going to be gone?" she asked as she made her way down the staircase.

He replied, "This station is going to be different. I never had to go anywhere in Rota. I'll be gone quite a bit here. You'll have Lula to keep you company though. She'll love the yard." Lula was a great companion. She'd been at the base kennel since Davin arrived in Italy.

"Speaking of Lula, we should go see her," said Lauren.

"I miss her." With that, Davin and Lauren locked up the house and headed back to the base to visit Lula before turning in for the evening. Moving day would be tiring, and they needed to rest.

By the end of her first week in Italy, Lauren and Davin were moved in and settled. Lula loved her new home too. Lauren and Davin spent the weekend preparing to report to each of their duty locations. Lauren wanted to check-in and meet the other AFN members she'd be working with for her reserve requirements, while Davin would be starting his new assignment with Sixth Fleet. There were three bases in Naples. AFN was located at the U.S. Naval Support Activity. This base was also referred to as the Support Site since housing, the schools, navy exchange, commissary, as well as a number of other support offices were all located on post. Davin's offices were located at U.S. Navy Base Capodichino. This base was adjacent to the Naples airport. Davin referred to it as Capo. Then there was the Allied Joint Force Command Naples. JFC Naples was the NATO post. Lauren wanted nothing to do with JFC. She was mortified there might come a time when she would have to visit for one reason or another.

On Monday morning, Lauren and Davin both got up and dressed in their uniforms. Davin pulled onto the Support Site to drop Lauren off. "I'll be back to pick you up later. It should be around seventeen hundred. Are you going to be alright until then," he asked.

Lauren assured him, "I'll be fine. I'll find something to do. Plus, I need a cell phone, and we need groceries. I'll call you once I have a number."

Lauren kissed him goodbye, exited the car, and watch as he drove away. She wasn't sure where the AFN building was located on post. She spotted a woman out for a stroll with her baby. Lauren politely asked for directions, and the woman happily directed her. Lauren was nervous as she entered the AFN building. She found the news studio, a few offices, and a radio booth on the first floor. The studio and offices were empty. Lauren looked through the window as she passed the lit-up radio booth. The 'On Air' sign was glowing, and the disc jockey was hard at work.

Lauren spotted a staircase at the end of the hall. Her heart was pounding as she went up. The second floor was noisier than the quiet emptiness of the first. Lauren popped her head into an open doorway. It was a news editing bay. Lauren noted there were six sailors and one airman. All were men.

Lauren interrupted, "Excuse me. Hi. I'm looking for the Senior Chief." Soon all eyes were on her. She understood. She was a uniformed stranger who had wandered in without an invitation. One sailor stood up from his computer and introduced himself.

"Hello, I'm Petty Officer Peter Shaw." Shaw offered his hand, and Lauren shook it.

"I'm Specialist Lauren Hendrix." He seemed cheerful and welcoming. He was also curious.

"The Senior Chief's office is this way."

Lauren followed him down the hall to Senior Chief Lucus' office.

"So, what brings you by?" he asked.

She answered, "I'm in the Army. Well, the reserves. I'll be working here from time to time."

They reached the Senior Chief's office, and Shaw announced, "Senior Chief, you have a visitor."

The Senior Chief looked up from his desk and said, "Hello, Specialist Mayer. I wasn't expecting you for a few weeks."

Lauren smiled. "Hello, Senior Chief," she responded.

"I just wanted to come by and say hi. Also, I thought it might be nice to meet everyone before I report for duty."

The Senior Chief was delighted to see her, and she was glad to see a familiar face. After they chatted for a bit, he led her back to the editing bay where he introduced her to everyone. They all seemed nice. Lauren could tell they'd been working together for a while. Their camaraderie was notable. The Senior Chief explained Lauren's presence to everyone. They all were receptive, and Lauren left confident she'd feel welcome among them. Lauren spent the remainder of her day wandering around the post. She also purchased a cell phone and called Davin to touch base. He didn't answer so, she left a message. "Hey, I'm headed over to the commissary. You can pick me up there. I love you! See you soon. Bye."

Lauren figured Davin was probably very busy, but he would be leaving soon. She was sure he'd listen to the message when he could. Eventually, Davin arrived at the support site and made his way to the commissary. When he finally found Lauren in the grocery aisle, she could tell he'd had an overwhelming first day. Lauren looked him over as he leaned on the end of the cart. "Hey, Shnuga Booga. How'd it go," she asked.

"It wasn't too bad," he replied. Lauren identified his optimistic demeanor and empathetically responded,

"Okay. You can tell me all about it on the way home." Lauren and Davin paid for their groceries and left the commissary. They each shared stories from their day as they drove to their house. After arriving, Lauren began cooking dinner while Davin unloaded the car.

Lauren and Davin adapted to their new environment quickly. Davin worked long hours and was deployed on a ship quite often. Lauren reported to AFN for her reserve duties. She even opted to volunteer many days just to be around other people for a bit and maintain her broadcast journalism skills. The guys at AFN embraced her presence wholeheartedly. They were very entertaining, and Lauren appreciated the friendships. Lauren also had Davin's car and a large beautiful home all to herself when he was away. These possessions were very appealing to the group of friends. The Army-Navy banter was hilarious too. Lauren felt blessed to have her boys. Together they explored the city, shared their victories, discussed their woes, and worked together as comrades and colleagues. When Davin was home, he'd join them on outings or at barbeques. They were all journalist, so Davin was a natural fit for the group. Plus, he was Lauren's husband. Some of her friends tolerated him while others genuinely liked him. Her boys were always loyal though, and she knew she could count on them.

Before Lauren had established these friendships, she was a mess of severe anxiety. She was always looking over her shoulder for Lieutenant Renzo. To her, he was just around every corner. When Davin was gone, her boys provided not only a distraction from this stress but also comfort and safety.

After a year of living in Italy, Lauren received an email from her command. She had orders to report to a month-long leadership course at Camp Ashland in Nebraska. The last place Lauren wanted to be was at Camp Ashland, especially since Davin would be returning from the ship soon. She hadn't seen much of him during their time in Italy. He'd met her friends on several occasions, but was still struggling with trust issues. Lauren was concerned about Davin's lack of confidence in her. However, she reassured him of her devotion to him as often as he needed her too. Between her perceived lurking monster and her worry over the status of their marriage, Lauren was struggling. She was more stressed than she'd ever been in her entire life. She began using red wine to self-medicate. After all, it was everywhere and very efficient at easing her anxiety. Lauren processed the information about the course. Perhaps it would not be so bad to take a break from Italy. Furthermore, completing the leadership course would make her eligible for a promotion to Sergeant. Lauren decided to embrace the situation positively.

Unfortunately, her command had only given her a few days' notice. The addition of an international flight narrowed her reporting window significantly. After looking at a calendar, Lauren realized there would be a week where both she and Davin would be gone. Lauren made arrangements for a dog sitter to care for Lula. She then sent an email to Davin since she could not call him when he was out at sea. Lauren was relieved when she received an email back from him acknowledging he'd gotten her news. Lauren notified her friends, packed her things, and purchased a one-way ticket. She'd be gone for at least a month. Lauren would sort out her return once she finished with her commitment stateside.

Lauren's month at Camp Ashland was grueling. The course was very intensive. It emphasized many different leadership topics, some of which were learned in the classroom while others were tested through practical application in the field. Despite the challenges, Lauren was in her element. She noticed how surprisingly relaxed she felt even though she was still concerned about Davin. Lauren was thankful when she received word he'd returned safely to care for Lula in her absence. However, she was also worried about how Davin would manage without her. He'd never been alone at the marble palace before. The house was lovely, but its size and the chill of the marble had a way of magnifying solitude. During their brief conversations, she recognized he did not seem like himself. He was lonely. Lauren desperately wanted to be with him but she also desperately wanted to cling to the peace that had settled over her mind. Leaving Italy had remedied a lot of Lauren's anxiety. She felt like weight had been removed from her shoulders and she appreciated it.

When the course wrapped up, Lauren bought herself a little more time stateside. One evening while speaking with Davin, she informed him she wanted to take an additional week to visit with her family in Texas before heading back to Italy. Davin agreed. This week turned into another, and before long Lauren had been in Texas a month. Davin was irritated with her, and he kept it no secret. They fought about her return to Naples almost every phone call. Lauren knew Davin felt hurt, perhaps even rejected. It wasn't that she didn't want to be with him. She just didn't want to be anywhere near Lieutenant Renzo. Lauren had to make a decision soon. She'd been gone a little over two months. She felt mentally tortured in Italy. She didn't want to go to Naples in the first place. Davin had decided upon the destination without consulting her. She'd moved there because she loved him so much, but at some point, Lauren had started to resent Davin. She hadn't realized the depth of this sentiment until she was away from the proximity of her monster. Lauren still hadn't told Davin about her assault. She hadn't told anyone, and it was slowly dissolving her mental well-being.

After a lot of reflection and prayer, Lauren decided to return to Naples. She couldn't allow her monster to conquer her sanity or affect the love she and Davin had found with each other. As Lauren packed her things and prepared to return to Naples to surprise her husband, she received a call from her friend, Shaw. Lauren answered, "Hey, buddy. What's up?"

Shaw informed her, "Hi, Lauren. I don't know what's going on between you and Davin, but you should know a girl named Jessica has been spending a lot of time with him. She was bragging about sleeping at your house the other day."

Shaw's words hit Lauren like a punch in the gut. "What? Who is Jessica?" she asked. Naturally, Davin had failed to mention a Jessica during their phone exchanges.

"She works with him over on Capo. She's public affairs. She was at one of my barbeques once." Lauren searched her mind. She had met a Jessica at Shaw's home many months before. The girl had gotten drunk and been very rude. At one point, she even grabbed another of the guests and proceeded to have sex with him in Shaw's bathroom. They were loud and unapologetic. It was disgusting.

"Wait. The bathroom sex girl," she asked. Shaw replied,

"Yup. That's the one." Lauren was appalled. Of all the people for Davin to misbehave with, he'd chosen the bathroom sex girl and allowed her to sleep in their home. Davin wasn't there when the bathroom sex occurred. He'd been on the ship. Lauren had mentioned it to him in conversation though. She had no idea this girl and Davin worked together.

Lauren responded, "Oh my God. Well, I'm headed back there today. I was going to surprise him. Thank you, Shaw. I'll see you soon."

Shaw apologized before hanging up, "I'm sorry, Lauren. Have a safe flight. I'll see you soon."

Lauren worried about her husband's affair the entire flight. It seemed she and Davin had emotionally distanced themselves from each other more than she'd realized. Lauren had essentially left him in Italy. Davin left her all the time and she hadn't strayed, but there had been a time prior to their marriage when she did seek comfort in another individual. Lauren disembarked in Rome for a short layover and turned on her phone. She had a new voicemail from another friend named, James Oliver. Oliver's message contained a description of Jessica's behavior following her and Davin's sleepover. Apparently, she'd been bragging about getting what she wanted and Davin was what she wanted. After listening to the second account of Davin's activities and Jessica's subsequent boasting, Lauren was hurt. Of course, her friends would be loyal.

Davin had been stupid to think the news wouldn't get back to her in such a small circle. Plus, Jessica's tacky mouth had done them no favors in the secret tryst department. Lauren wondered if divine intervention had influenced her timely arrival. She suddenly felt a desperate need to be home with her husband. Davin didn't know that Lauren had found out about his activities, or that she'd learned about them when she was in route to preserve their marriage. Lauren called Davin while she waited to board her next flight. She did not want to address Jessica over the phone, but was curious what his reaction would be to her surprise return.

When he answered she said, "Hey, It's me. Your wife, Lauren."

Lauren listened for his response. "I know," he said.

She asked, "Are you at work?" Davin replied, "Yes. Why?"

"Surprise. I just landed in Rome."

Lauren continued, "You can pick me up when I land in Naples, or I can walk over to Capo and meet you there."

Davin was silent for a moment. The next words out of his mouth were not ones of relief, but rather dismay. "You're in Rome? Lauren, why didn't you tell me you were coming back?"

Lauren responded, "Because I wanted to surprise you. Besides, I am your wife. I can come home to my husband if I want to." Davin agreed to pick her up, and they hung up the phone. There was definitely palpable tension between them.

Lauren landed in Naples and called Davin again to let him know she arrived. She waited outside the airport about ten minutes before he pulled up to retrieve her. Neither of them was overjoyed to see each other, and the car ride home was relatively silent. When they arrived, Lula met them with glee. Lauren patted her on the head and unloaded her suitcase as Davin unlocked the house. When Lauren stepped through the front door, she immediately noticed that Davin had taken down every photo of her or them together. Lauren who had been trying to remain diplomatic until she could address Jessica was suddenly enraged.

She turned to Davin and furiously asked, "Where are the pictures? Did you take them down so that bitch would feel more comfortable in our home?"

The color drained from Davin's face.

Lauren went on, "Yup! I know all about it. Where are my pictures?" Davin walked over to the buffet in their dining room and opened a drawer where he had stashed them. He pulled them out and handed them to her.

Lauren proceeded to hang them all back up as she yelled, "What the fuck, Davin!"

Davin yelled back, "You left me!"

Lauren was angry, "I did not leave you. I was on orders. Then I visited my family. I was only gone two months."

The arguing continued for several hours. Jessica was only one of many things Lauren was upset about. She did not need any more details about his slumber party. She was hurt enough. Lauren always kept her disgruntled feelings to herself, and she constantly gave into Davin's whims because she cared for him so much. She went along with his will even when conceding meant she felt isolated and crazy. If he only knew how difficult it was for her to be in Naples, he might understand, but he didn't. Lauren had even tagged along once with him to JFC when he requested it of her. She'd been supportive and loving and agreeable despite her inner turmoil. In return, he'd erased her from their home to make his flirtation comfortable.

That evening Lauren put on lingerie and slept in the guest bedroom alone. She liked wearing lingerie when she was sick or sad. The delicate material had a way of making her feel beautiful when she felt unpleasant. Plus, Lauren wanted Davin to eat his heart out. She proceeded to spend the next few days dressed this way. She also continued to sleep in the guest bedroom. Lauren and Davin had said a lot of hurtful things during their fight. They had not made up either. It was awkward living in the same space afterward. All the feelings they'd not dealt with had finally come to a head. During their epic argument, they vented every raw emotion they had on each other. She and Davin had never fought like that before. After a week, they still hadn't touched and had hardly spoken to one another. Lauren wasn't sure what to do next. She was heartbroken and wondered if perhaps this was what she deserved as payback for Peters.

One sleepless night as she stared at the ceiling, Davin silently came into her room. Lauren moved from the middle of the bed, and Davin crawled under the covers next to her. Lauren took his hand in hers. She realized it was the first physical contact they'd shared since their fight.

As they both proceeded to stare upward, Davin asked, "Should we go to marital counseling?"

Lauren released his hand and turned onto her side to face him. "It couldn't hurt," she said. Davin rolled onto his side and placed his forehead against hers.

"I'm sorry."

She replied, "I'm sorry too."

Davin continued, "I just thought you were never…"

Lauren interrupted, "Shhhhh." She placed her index finger to his lips. "I'm afraid we'll argue again. I don't want to argue right now." Davin nodded and kissed her finger.

Lauren removed it and kissed him lovingly on the mouth. Then she whispered, "Make love to your wife." Davin slowly placed his hand beneath the lace of Lauren's nightgown and exposed her breast. She closed her eyes to focus on the sensation of her tension gradually succumbing to the pleasure of his touch. Davin kissed her chest and danced his tongue across her erect nipple. Lauren, overcome with her desire, pushed him onto his back and mounted him. As she inserted his hard cock into her wet vagina, she was reminded of how beautifully they fit together.

It was as if God had specifically designed them for each other. Lauren rocked her hips against his while Davin watched. Breathlessly she leaned in to kiss him. His firm chest against the softness of hers was titillating. Lauren's mouth lingered at his lips for a moment before returning to an upright position. Davin's penis felt as though it were touching the depths of her soul. He placed his hands on her hips and pulled her against him to penetrate her further. Lauren moaned with every exquisite sensation. As she began to climax, she slowed her rocking. Davin instructed, "Don't stop." To help her maintain her rhythm, he began to pull and push her hips against him. Suddenly Davin announced, "Lauren, I'm cumming." Both of their orgasms were intense and prolonged. When they'd both finished, Lauren collapsed on top of him. Davin remained inserted as she caught her breath.

"I love you," said Lauren. Davin played with her hair as she laid on top of his chest.

"I love you too, Lauren. Tomorrow I'll call someone to help us."

Lauren replied, "Okay." No matter what had happened, it was apparent they had something special, and Lauren was hopeful they could work it out.

Lauren and Davin began marital counseling. There was a lot to navigate. Married life moving forward wasn't always easy. They fought a lot, but they also made an effort to kiss and make up. They talked more too. It wasn't perfect, but Lauren and Davin were working together to fix their marriage. Lauren had also begun to seriously consider telling Davin about Lieutenant Renzo. Their therapy sessions provided a neutral and safe environment for her to do so, but every time Lauren worked up the courage to address it she'd change her mind mid-session. Lauren's friends became her family throughout it all. Since Jessica had run her mouth, they all knew what had occurred. Jessica attempted to befriend Lauren's friends. She said terrible things about Lauren to anyone who would listen. She also confronted Lauren once as if Lauren were somehow wrong for loving Davin enough to try and save their marriage. Lauren's friends always promptly notified her of Jessica's toxic and trashy behavior. Lauren wasn't keen on knowing every detail. In fact, she wished the woman would get over her husband and go away. Lauren's friends were always quick to defend her when Jessica offered the opportunity. Her boys were like her brothers. She could talk to Shaw or Oliver about anything. They were kind and provided a male perspective which she appreciated. Since the group was small, Lauren requested no one take sides. Her friends, while loyal to her, made an effort to include Davin in activities and events. They were skeptical at times, but supportive of their decision to work it out. After several months, it seemed like she and Davin would survive this rocky ordeal.

One evening while attending a friendly game of Texas Hold 'em at Shaw's home, Lauren received a call from her Commander. Davin had given Lauren a quick rundown before the game, but she really didn't know how to play. She was losing miserably. Lauren was relieved for the interruption and excused herself from the table to step out and take the call.

"Hello, Specialist Hendrix. It's Major Rodrick."

Lauren replied, "Hello, Major."

The Major continued, "I'm contacting you to inform you, you've been cross-leveled to a unit in Birmingham, Alabama. They are deploying to AFN - Iraq."

Lauren processed the information, "AFN - Iraq? Why me?"

The Major responded, "I'm not sure. They asked for you specifically. You have orders."

Lauren had received first place in the Rising Star category of the LTC Wetzel Brumfield Excellence in Journalism for her broadcast products during her time at AFN - Iraq. She wondered if this award had anything to do with it.

"Alright. Can you email me a copy of the orders?" she asked.

The Major confirmed, "I sure can. Have a nice evening."

Lauren thanked her for the call and hung up the phone. She sat down in a chair on Shaw's porch. Lauren and Davin had worked so hard to remain together. While they had managed to improve their relationship, they still had a lot to sort through. Lauren didn't want to leave her husband now. She knew their marriage wouldn't survive a year of separation, especially after all that had taken place. Lauren returned to her husband's side. Everyone was having a wonderful time while Lauren silently worried about the impact of an impending deployment on her marriage. She also worried about her own state of mind. Her last deployment in Iraq had been traumatic. She had hoped she'd never set foot in the country ever again, but it seemed that would not be the case. Lauren decided not to mention it to Davin until the next day. They'd have a lot to talk about, and now was not the time or the place.

Chapter 12

Lauren and Davin discussed her orders to Birmingham and deployment back to Iraq. They were both uneasy and acknowledged the implications it would have on their marriage. Lauren felt like they'd finally stumbled upon the beginning of the end. Sorrowfully, Lauren packed her things. There was no point in leaving her belongings behind for Davin to deal with. She and Davin discussed what would stay and what would go. After they agreed, movers came to collect her items and ship them back to Texas. Her whole life would be packed away in a storage unit again. Lauren felt heartbroken. Neither had mentioned divorce, but the preparations they were making felt just like one. When her belongings were gone, so was she. Davin dropped her at the airport and Lauren boarded her flight. She would spend a week with her family and then she'd be off to Birmingham.

Lauren arrived in Texas. It was September. Her family was happy to see her, but she could find no joy. Not even a small birthday celebration cheered her up. She was deploying again with a group of strangers to a war zone she'd been in before. Bad things had happened to her there. She'd almost lost Davin there. As the week marched on, she became an increasing mess of anxiety and fear. Lauren knew their relationship probably wouldn't survive another separation. She spent the entire week secretly downing tequila and receding further into sadness.

Finally, the day came for her to fly to Birmingham. She was met at the airport by one of the other soldiers from the unit. Together they drove to the detachment's training location. When she arrived, she was given a training schedule. Lauren was the last soldier to report, and there was no time to waste. As Lauren made her way into a classroom and found a seat, she immediately noticed many of the soldiers were very young. Their ranks indicated they'd more than likely just graduated basic training. Only a handful outranked her. Lauren's stress level began to increase.

The class in progress was a combat lifesaver course. This training covered critical first aid and trauma care procedures. During a break, the instructor pulled up a video on the projector screen to share with the class. It showed an improvised explosive device being detonated as a military convoy passed. The younger soldiers shouted expletives, made sarcastic remarks, and laughed. None of the individuals of higher rank said or did anything to quell this behavior. The instructor further encouraged the privates by proceeding to the next awful bit of footage, repeating another round of the same shocking commentary. Lauren was enraged. Combat first aid and the violent attacks that made the knowledge necessary were serious matters. Lauren found the instructor's lack of professionalism appalling. Moreover, how could she trust these inexperienced children who apparently found watching these horrific real-life scenes entertaining.

Lauren couldn't stand it anymore and stood up to leave the room. Seeing this, the instructor paused the video and asked, "You alright, Specialist Hendrix?"

Lauren stopped, pointed at the screen, and sternly reprimanded, "That is footage of fellow service members being attacked by evil men in a country we're about to deploy to for a year. People like us record that kind of footage. Many of those individuals are likely severely wounded, or possibly even dead from that explosion. Men and women just like you and me with families. Have some respect."

Lauren turned and left the room. She had reached her limit. As she found the women's bathroom and entered, her heart was pounding. Lauren was having a nervous breakdown. She still hadn't dealt with her monster or any of the other stressors from her first deployment. The dissolution of her marriage seemed imminent. She was deploying with a bunch of immature children she didn't know or trust. Also, she'd just thrown a very inappropriate fit in front of a classroom full of soldiers, some of whom outranked her. Lauren splashed her face with water and sat down on a chair next to the bathroom sink. When she didn't return to the classroom, a female Sergeant was sent to look for her. She entered the bathroom and found Lauren lost in thought, sitting with her elbows propped on her knees, and her head in her hands.

She asked, "Specialist, are you okay?"

Lauren wasn't, and she didn't know what to say to this stranger. She replied, "I don't think so."

The Sergeant continued, "The Commander would like to see you in his office." Lauren should have known someone would run and tattle on her. She hadn't met her new Commander yet, but her outburst had gotten her an immediate audience. She was sure he'd reprimand her. Lauren was proud of her spotless military record. Her outburst would probably tarnish it a little.

She laughed and apologized to the Sergeant, "I'm sorry. I guess I gave one heck of a first impression." Lauren stood and exited the bathroom to make her way to a waiting Major whom she assumed was not very pleased with her at the moment.

Lauren and the female Sergeant entered the Commander's office. He instructed them to take seats. Lauren nervously complied.

Major Thomas Dailey looked her over before asking, "What seems to be the problem, Specialist Hendrix?" Lauren was at her wit's end.

She was tired of pretending she was alright and replied, "I'm not okay. I think I need to talk to someone? Maybe some medication might help? I don't know anymore."

The Commander was kind about her admission. "Alright then. I'll have Sergeant Evert take you to Maxwell to talk to someone. You're dismissed."

Lauren and Sergeant Evert exited the Commander's office and immediately headed to Maxwell Air Force Base in Montgomery, Alabama. While there, Lauren spoke with a psychologist. She told him about her excessive drinking and the worries currently plaguing her mind. As always, she omitted her assault. Adding it to her pile of woes wouldn't have made much difference anyway. The psychologist instructed a waiting Sergeant Evert to immediately take Lauren to an emergency room for further evaluation and care. After hearing these orders, Lauren became further unsettled. Her nervous breakdown and request for medication had won her nothing but more anxiety.

Lauren and Sergeant Evert traveled to the ER as directed. When they arrived, she was checked in and placed in a room to wait. Lauren and Sergeant Evert were exchanging small chat when suddenly there was a terrible commotion in the room next to hers. Lauren could see a patient who appeared to be having issues screaming and swinging his fists at nurses. A woman who was with him was crying. Lauren gathered she was his mother and that he had schizophrenia from the information the woman was shouting to the medical personnel actively trying to restrain him. A doctor finally arrived and sedated him. Lauren was in tears after watching this. She wasn't crazy yet here she was waiting to be seen by the same doctor. She was scared. Lauren wasn't sure what would happen to her next.

When the doctor finally came in, he informed her, "The psychologist who sent you over here called, and talked to us. He's faxing his report here and to your command. He is recommending observation. I'm going to call your Commander and let him know that I am recommending observation as well."

Lauren was terrified. She didn't know what this would mean for her military standing.

"Observation? Are you committing me? I'm not crazy," she said bluntly.

"No, you're not. But there is cause for concern given your state of mind and your future deployment situation. You can volunteer to commit yourself, or you can leave, in which case, your command will have you committed involuntarily."

Lauren sat in silence. There was no way she was going to be able to walk out of this hospital. Her request for medication and the information she'd shared with the psychologist had placed her on the fast track to the looney bin, and Lauren hadn't even shared the worst of it.

She asked, "Where will I go? I won't be with him, will I?"

Lauren pointed toward the sedated patient's room. The doctor replied, "No, there are different floors for different levels of psychiatric care."

"I don't need psychiatric care," she insisted.

"We think you do," he replied. Lauren was tired both physically and emotionally. It had been a long day that started with an airport and would end with a mental institution. She took a deep breath and conceded. Lauren signed the necessary paperwork, and the doctor transferred her to the hospital's psychiatric facility. When Lauren arrived at the psychiatric floor's intake station, the nurse stripped her of her clothing, took her vitals, and inspected her naked body thoroughly to ensure she wasn't smuggling hazards. Lauren felt she was being treated like a felon processing into the prison system. She was too tired to protest anymore. She put on the purple scrubs she was given and followed the nurse to a room. It was empty except for an open bathroom and a bed. Lauren made her way over to the bed and crawled in. The nurse offered her a sleeping pill which Lauren thankfully accepted. When the nurse left, Lauren pondered the sequence of events that had transpired in such a short period. She couldn't believe asking for help had led to her being committed. It had been several days since she'd slept well and she was truly exhausted. Lauren wasn't awake much longer. The medication quickly began to take effect, and she fell asleep.

In the morning, a nurse came to wake Lauren to take her vitals. Afterward, she asked, "Are you hungry? Breakfast is being served in the dining hall." Lauren wasn't hungry, but she didn't want to sit in her room all day. She needed information. She had no idea how long she was expected to stay at this facility.

Lauren asked, "Where is it?" The nurse smiled and gave her directions. Lauren wandered out of her room and noted the floor's layout. It was simple, and she found the dining room easily. The staff monitoring breakfast asked Lauren for her name and found her tray. She took it and sat down at an empty table. Lauren was picking at her meal when she looked up and noticed a man entering the room. She recognized him immediately. He was the violent schizophrenic from the ER. The doctor had told her they wouldn't be on the same floor. However, here he was collecting his tray. Lauren watched him as he made his way over to her table. They made eye contact as he sat down across from her. Lauren was worried. She averted her eyes and picked up her juice box.

The man leaned toward the middle of the table and whispered, "I know who you are."

Lauren didn't want to talk to him and remained silent. He insisted, "I know you. I do. You can see the future." Then he sat back in his seat and sang in a creepy lilt,

"I know who you are." He followed this with an outburst of, "Juicy Box!" Lauren pulled the straw of her juice box from her lips and looked at the packaging. Then she looked at him. He was insane, but he could read.

Lauren was disturbed, but calmly offered, "I can't see the future." This statement seemed to anger him.

"That's a lie, Juicy Box," he replied.

Lauren pushed her chair back from the table and said, "Please excuse me." She returned her tray and left the dining room. The whole exchange had been unnerving. It didn't stop with her exit though. For several hours he continued to bother her.

Every time he saw Lauren, he would sing 'Juicy Box' in a creepy lilt. When lunchtime came, he found her again sitting alone. Lauren didn't understand why he'd zeroed in on her. He sat down and demanded, "Juicy Box, tell me my future!"

Again, Lauren calmly informed him, "I can't see the future."

Enraged, he slammed both his fists on the table and said, "I'm gonna kill you!" Lauren had witnessed this man's fury the night before. She knew what he was capable of. Lauren promptly stood up and marched past the nurses who were making their way over to calm him. When she reached the nurse's station, she was upset and forcefully knocked on the window.

She demanded, "I want to talk to a doctor right now! I do not need to be here. I'm not even from Alabama. I'm from Texas, and I'm not crazy!" A male nurse grabbed her from behind pinning her arms to her side. Lauren turned her head to see the individual who was hanging on to her.

Infuriated further she yelled, "Why are you restraining me? Let me go! I haven't done anything wrong."

Out of nowhere, a doctor appeared with a syringe. He plugged the needle into Lauren's arm.

"This is an injection of Ativan to calm you," he said. He was right about the drug's calming effect. It wasn't long before the Ativan's intended purpose of sedation washed over her. The events that took place next were very foggy. In fact, Lauren had immense difficulty recalling most of it later.

Lauren opened her eyes. She was lying in a different room than the one she had been in before. She sat up and looked around. She was very confused. Lauren vaguely remembered standing in an airport, in front of large windows, watching a plane pull up. It seemed like Sergeant Evert may have been there, but she couldn't be sure. Lauren wasn't positive if the recollection was a memory or a dream. Disoriented, she stood and exited the room she was in. Everything looked different. She wondered if they had moved her to another floor because of her fit.

Lauren found a nurse and asked, "Where am I?"

The nurse looked at her compassionately and said, "Dear, you're in Texas."

Lauren stood in silence for a moment. If this woman was joking, Lauren wasn't amused. She inquired, "Texas? Where in Texas?"

The nurse chuckled a bit at her skepticism. "You're in Killeen, Texas at the Metroplex Behavioral Health Center. Let me get your file," she said. Lauren thanked her and waited while the nurse glanced over a manila folder full of paperwork.

She continued, "Let's see. You came in late last night. You were transferred here from a facility in Alabama. You were medicated when you arrived. Oh, we still need your next of kin information."

Lauren realized she had not contacted anyone in her family to inform them of her hospitalization. She thought about it. Lauren's initial impulse was to list Davin, but there was nothing he could do from Italy, so she provided her mother's contact information instead.

She then asked, "May I call her?"

The nurse responded, "Sure thing," and dialed the number before handing her the phone.

Lauren's mother answered, "Hello."

She replied, "Hey, mom. I'm in Killeen."

"Thank God," she said. "Lauren, when you called before you did not sound anything like yourself. You were really out of it. You joked about going crazy in Alabama before laughing hysterically and hanging up."

Lauren asked, "I did?" She honestly did not remember calling or speaking with her mother. Crazy in Alabama was one of their favorite movies. Lauren found it funny she'd made the joke, but troubled by the fact she did not remember the interaction.

"I know they gave me Ativan, but I don't really remember anything after that. I had a nervous breakdown. I'm pretty sure I'm not fit for duty," she said.

Lauren's mother continued, "The Commander in Alabama called Major Rodrick. She called us. He's going to release you and send your belongings to her. Major Rodrick said not to worry about anything and to get better."

Lauren had left all her things in Alabama. She hadn't anticipated when she set out for Maxwell that she wouldn't be back.

"Okay," Lauren said.

"Could you call Davin?" Lauren's mother confirmed she would call him before saying goodbye and hanging up.

Lauren was glad she was back in Texas. However, she was not happy she was trapped in a mental health facility. Lauren desperately wanted to be released and adamantly informed the staff she did not need to be there. It took three days, several medications, and multiple groups and individual therapy sessions to realize, yes, she did indeed need to be exactly where she was. Plus, being stubborn and uncooperative was only further proving she was not well. Lauren swallowed her pride and accepted her situation. She had been struggling for some time and needed to develop healthier coping skills. Being away from Davin and Italy gave her the distance she needed to focus on herself. It had been a long time since Lauren had been able to concentrate on her needs. She had changed drastically due to her experiences and used Davin as a diversion to keep from dealing with her own demons. Pretending to be the version of herself he'd fallen in love with hadn't done them any favors either. She was a different person. After two weeks of monitoring and therapy, her psychiatrist and command agreed she could be released to her sister, Judy. Major Rodrick insisted she stay in Texas to continue her weekly counseling sessions and Lauren agreed.

Lauren called Davin to let him know what she'd decided. Lauren's mother had spoken with him periodically during her commitment, but Lauren had not. She wasn't sure how he would take the news, but she needed to attend to her mental well-being through continued counseling.

Davin answered, "Hey, baby. How are you?" Lauren chatted with him for a bit. She shared some stories from her time at both facilities. He especially got a kick out of the juice box obsessed schizophrenic. At the time, it had been terrifying, but as she retold the story, she even laughed.

Finally, Lauren came to a place in conversation to segway her next thoughts. "Listen, Davin. I think I'm going to stay in Texas for a while. I need to get better and stay better." Davin was silent for a moment.

Then he said, "I'm relieved your family stepped in to care for you. I'm gone a lot. Let's face it. Things were really rough between us here." Lauren shouldn't have felt hurt, but she was. Davin had promised to take care of her when he talked her into their Justice of the Peace marriage. She felt like Davin was telling her he was glad someone else had stepped in to do his job. Lauren was disheartened but pretended to be unfazed. She did not want to have this potential snowball of a conversation over the phone, so she said goodbye and hung up. Lauren thought about her relationship with Davin. She'd made many sacrifices for him. She'd even put her sanity on the line. In therapy, Lauren learned many useful tools to utilize moving forward, but she still had so much to work out. Davin was a distraction to her healing process. Lauren wasn't sure where their relationship would go from here, but she was sure he'd be another subject of conversation for therapy.

Chapter 13

Lauren and Davin kept their conversations light and amicable through the end of the year. While they were separated, Lauren moved in with Judy in San Marcos. Judy and Cliff had recently broken up and she had a spare bedroom in her apartment. It was a convenient temporary arrangement that allowed Lauren to continue attending her weekly therapy sessions. She missed Davin immensely but remained dedicated to fixing the parts of her that felt broken. She and Davin spoke often. During one phone call, Davin informed Lauren he would be leaving Italy at the end of January for another stint at sea. Lauren was glad he was staying busy and happy she wasn't in Italy to be left alone once again. When she asked if he could return stateside for a visit, he confirmed he had plans to see her before boarding the ship. Lauren's excitement grew as she counted down the days to her husband's arrival.

Davin landed safely in Texas the first week of January. Since he'd flown into Dallas Fort Worth International Airport and Lauren lived in San Marcos, they agreed to meet at a shopping mall in Waco. Waco was halfway, more or less, for both of them. When Davin met her, Lauren noticed his demeanor was different. He seemed distant and unaffectionate. As they walked through the mall, Lauren wondered what was going on with him. She thought it might be nerves.

After all, they had been separated for a few months. Lauren grew worried and asked, "Is there something wrong?" Davin took her hand and led her over to a bench where they both sat down.

He replied, "Lauren, I've been thinking about a lot of things, and I've decided I want a divorce." Davin's words were heavy. So much so, Lauren thought they might crush her heart. She looked away to process what she'd just heard.

She and Davin had made vows to each other. He'd promised "for better or worse" and "in sickness and in health." Lauren had kept her promises to him, but now that it was his turn to keep his, he wanted to abandon ship. She suspected their union might end in divorce. She had also hoped and prayed with all her heart that the love they shared was enough to preserve their marriage.

"A divorce? I don't want a divorce," she said.

He continued, "I do though. I don't know where we go from here. I don't take this lightly."

Lauren was hurt. Davin didn't want to be her husband anymore. Her feelings of rejection were intense, and Lauren thought she would cry. She was barely hanging on to her tears when Davin landed another blow.

"I had JAG prepare the divorce papers. I have them with me. I'd like to file them together while I'm here." Lauren could no longer keep the tears back.

"You've got the papers with you," she asked in disbelief. Davin nodded in affirmation, and Lauren sighed heavily in response.

Lauren had bent over backward for Davin. She'd blamed herself when he was upset. She'd gone along with things that made her miserable for his contentment. She'd lost her sanity to spare his. She'd cheered on every accomplishment and supported every whim as the dutiful wife she felt he deserved. Through it all, pieces of her had been slowly chiseled away to accommodate his wants and needs. Now Lauren realized while she had been working diligently to regain her footing, Davin had been making preparations to knock her flat and leave her when she needed him most. Lauren suddenly felt defeated. Once again, she would find herself stashing her own emotions and giving into Davin.

"Fine," she said as she wept. She wanted him to be happy so much she was willing to sacrifice her own happiness. Lauren stood up from the bench. She was distraught and uncertain she could safely operate a vehicle.

"Let's go to the courthouse. You drive," she said.

Davin responded, "Okay." He took her hand as they exited the mall and led her through the parking lot to his truck. It was odd and confusing. Here they were about to make the heart-wrenching accommodations to dissolve their marriage yet they were still exchanging comforting affectionate gestures.

Davin and Lauren drove toward the courthouse. Along the way, she tired of looking out the window and laid her head in his lap. As she rested her hand and cheek against her husband's thigh, she could feel him becoming aroused beneath his blue jeans. Soon Davin was fully erect.

Lauren looked up at him. "Sorry," he said.

She smiled and joked, "Are you sure you want a divorce?" From the first day they met, Lauren and Davin had shared an inexplicable electric connection. Through all their ups and downs, this tingling magnetism was continually present and always pulled them back together. Their attraction was strong, and denying their bond was impossible. Davin pulled the truck over and killed the engine. Lauren moved her hand from its place on his thigh, unbuttoned, and unzipped his jeans. Then she pulled his firm penis from beneath the fabric and kissed it tenderly as she looked up at him.

Davin let her linger for a moment before requesting, "Can we get in the backseat?" Lauren was reminded of the insatiable appetite they'd had for each other when they first started dating. She complied by crawling into the backseat. Lauren situated herself on her hands and knees while Davin positioned himself behind her. He then pulled her skirt up, moved the crotch of her panties aside, and accommodated himself inside of her. There in the light of day, at a roadside park, he took her forcefully. The sex was so spontaneous, thrilling, and charged with emotion that neither one took long to cum. It was a quickie and an exhilarating one at that. Afterward, they silently straightened out their clothing before returning to their mission.

Lauren and Davin arrived at the courthouse and located the District Clerk's office. The clerk informed them there would be a sixty-day waiting period before a judge could finalize their divorce. Lauren and Davin signed all the necessary papers and filed them. The first available date was March nineteenth. Lauren programmed it into her cell phone's calendar. She would have to attend alone since Davin would be on a ship overseas. Lauren wasn't looking forward to it but promised Davin she would be present at the proceedings to make sure their final decree was accepted and filed.

It was difficult for her to imagine not being his anymore after sharing five years of their lives together, especially after the sex they'd just had. Naturally, Lauren was emotionally overwhelmed. When they were done, Davin returned Lauren to the mall and dropped her off at her car.

She kissed his cheek and said, "I love you, Shnuga Booga," before exiting his vehicle. Lauren didn't know at the moment, but it would be the last time she'd ever kiss him.

Lauren promptly left Waco and headed back to San Marcos. She desperately needed to vent to her sister, but Judy wasn't home when she arrived. Lauren laid down on the couch and cried into the cushion. Judy found her there when she returned. She knew Lauren had met Davin and asked, "What happened?" Lauren sat up and recounted the details. Judy had grown to dislike Davin and made it no secret. "What a piece of shit," she said. Lauren didn't like it when Judy said things like this about Davin, but she was entitled to her opinion. In Lauren's heartbroken state she found it oddly comforting. Lauren sat up so Judy could sit down on the couch next to her. "I need wine and ice cream," said Lauren.

Judy hugged her tight, "Come on then. Let's go get you some supplies." The next few weeks were rough for Lauren as she struggled with the acceptance of her divorce. She looked at her phone's calendar every day. Unlike her and Davin's other countdowns, this one was torture.

One day while staring at dates, Lauren realized her period was late. Her time of the month was another event she tracked. She tended to be irregular and took birth control pills not only to prevent pregnancy but also keep her cycle regular. In an effort to keep track of her many prescribed medications, Lauren had taken to using a large pillbox instead of retrieving the pills from their individual packaging on a daily basis. Unfortunately, Lauren had also been extraordinarily distracted by events in her life. She made her way to the bathroom medicine cabinet to look at her birth control pill pack. Lauren opened it to reveal a practically filled pack. She realized she'd forgotten to include them the last few times she refilled the pillbox. Lauren quickly rectified the situation. She wasn't immediately concerned, but as her week progressed, she began to fret about her oversight.

Lauren, doubtful she was pregnant, needed to pee on a stick to ease her mind and decided to purchase a pregnancy test. She read the directions and did as they instructed. After a few nerve-racking minutes, Lauren had her answer. The test indicated it was positive. She sat down on the edge of the bathtub in disbelief. She had fully convinced herself the test would be negative and afterward she'd carry on, worry-free with her day. Lauren buried the evidence in the wastebasket and exited the bathroom to make an appointment with her primary care provider. She wasn't entirely convinced and wanted an examination to verify the accuracy of the results.

Lauren called her Doctor's office to request an appointment, and they were able to accommodate her quickly. While there, Dr. Mitchell confirmed she was, in fact, expecting although it was still very early. Lauren hadn't slept with anyone other than Davin. Based on this information, her doctor estimated she was a little over a month along. Lauren was concerned about her prescriptions and the effect they might have on her developing fetus.

She asked, "Should I just quit taking everything?"

Dr. Mitchell went through her chart, "Lauren, you're on quite a few medications. We'll need to start tapering you off." Lauren discussed her medical options with the doctor and decided she'd proceed with a tapering regimen. Dr. Mitchell provided the names of a few obstetricians and sent her on her way with prenatal vitamins. Lauren spent the next two weeks processing her pregnancy. She was going to have Davin's baby. She was also set to divorce him in a month. The timing of it all was terrible. Lauren had a lot to think about including whether or not she should tell Davin. This dilemma would eventually resolve itself.

One evening while Lauren and Judy watched TV, she began to feel sharp pains in her lower abdomen. Lauren readjusted herself to ease these cramps, but they persisted. She soon lost focus in the program they were watching and began to become increasingly concerned by what she was experiencing. Suddenly, Lauren felt dampness in her underwear. She quietly got up and went to the bathroom. There she discovered she was bleeding. Lauren removed her bloodied clothing and called out to her sister, "Judy, I'm bleeding. There's something wrong."

Lauren hadn't shared her news with Judy yet.

Judy came to the bathroom door and asked, "What do you mean? Do you need a tampon?"

Lauren suspected she was having a miscarriage and responded, "No. Do you have a pad? I think I'm having a miscarriage." This is not how Lauren had intended to share her news, but there was a developing situation. She could no longer keep her secret. Lauren heard Judy run up the stairs to her bathroom to retrieve a pad.

She quickly returned and shouted through the closed door, "I'm coming in, Lauren."

Lauren was sitting on the toilet when Judy entered. "A miscarriage," Judy asked.

Lauren replied, "Yes. I went to the doctor, and I'm pregnant."

"Oh my God, Lauren. Why didn't you tell me?"

Judy was upset. Lauren admitted, "I haven't told Davin. I haven't known what to do."

Judy said, "You need to go to the emergency room. I'll get my keys."

As she exited the bathroom, Lauren hollered, "I'm not going to the emergency room."

Judy returned and asked, "What do you mean? You need to go."

Lauren explained, "I'm not that far along. Going to the emergency room now is not going to stop the cramps or the bleeding. I'll call my doctor first thing in the morning. If it gets any worse, I promise I'll let you take me to the ER."

Judy didn't like it but agreed. Lauren threw her soiled clothing in the trash. After showering, she laid down. Judy, still concerned, tucked her in and demanded, "Promise me you'll call your doctor in the morning!" Lauren promised and tried to get some rest.

The next morning Lauren called her doctor's office. One of his nurses returned her call and requested she come in as soon as possible. Lauren arrived at the office. After she checked in, a nurse escorted her to a room where Dr. Mitchell performed a pelvic examination and an ultrasound to verify she'd had a miscarriage.

"Lauren, I'm sorry. Sometimes it just happens this way," he said.

Lauren was upset. She'd lost Davin's baby. The confirmation of what she already suspected was difficult to hear.

"I know," she replied.

Lauren returned home afterward. Judy was waiting for her when she walked through the door.

She asked, "So?"

Lauren answered, "I lost the baby." These words prompted a waterfall of tears. Lauren could no longer contain her feelings of loss.

She'd grown excited over the few weeks she'd known. Now, the life she and Davin had created was gone.

Judy hugged Lauren. "I'm very sorry, Lauren." Lauren blamed herself for the miscarriage.

She cried harder as she said, "It's my fault. Maybe I was too stressed. Maybe it was the medications. Maybe it's me. The doctor said these things happen, but I think it was me."

"I think you need to rest now," said Judy. Lauren nodded in agreement and made her way to her room.

Judy came to check on Lauren after a while. Worried, she sat down on the edge of her bed and asked, "Are you going to tell Davin?"

Consumed by sadness, Lauren replied, "What's the point? It doesn't change anything. We're divorcing."

Judy continued, "You are always trying to spare him. Why? He's a jerk. I'd tell him. You don't deserve to go through this alone."

Judy made a valid point.

She reached for Lauren's phone on her bedside table and handed it to her insisting, "Call him!"

"He's on the ship right now," said Lauren.

Judy continued, "Then leave him a message." Lauren dialed the number. It went to voicemail like she knew it would.

After she heard the beep, Lauren sorrowfully reported, "Davin, I don't know how to tell you this so I'll just say it. I was pregnant, but I had a miscarriage. The baby was ours. I'm sorry to leave this news as a message. I'm sorry I lost our child."

Lauren was weeping when she hung up. She looked at Judy who was still sitting on her bed.

"Done," she said as she set the phone back on her bedside table. Judy seemed pleased. Lauren hated the fact she'd left such sad information the way she did, but relieved to share her grief with Davin. Judy was right. Lauren and Davin had created a life together. It was unfair for her to have to bear the pain of loss alone. At one time, she and Davin had talked about creating a family together. The divorce had dashed this dream. Although complicated, the discovery of her pregnancy felt like a blessing. Lauren's miscarriage was tremendously upsetting to her. She also felt like it was another nail in their relationship's coffin.

Several days passed before Lauren received a return phone call from Davin. After they exchanged a few cordial words, Davin apologized, "Lauren, I'm sorry I didn't get back to you right away. I called as soon as I could. We just got back to port."

Lauren understood and replied, "I figured as much." She had been a mess of sadness and didn't know what to say to him.

Davin continued, "I guess this is for the best? I don't know. It hit me hard. I cried."

Lauren was touched to hear this even though it was an awful way to establish he cared.

"I'm sorry, Davin," she said.

"It was bad enough to lose you, but then I lost our baby too. Sometimes I wish we could start over."

Davin's voice wavered as he spoke, "Me too. I heard a song that reminded me of us today." He recited a few of the lyrics, and Lauren recognized it.

It was a familiar one by Rascal Flatts titled 'What Hurts The Most'. "That's a sad song," she said.

Davin replied, "I know."

Lauren offered information by asking, "Would you like to know what happened?"

Davin replied, "Yes, if it's not too painful for you to tell me." It was painful, but Lauren thought he should know the details. She began recounting the sequence of events that led to her discovery of the pregnancy and her thoughts after the miscarriage. Davin asked lots of questions, and Lauren answered. They hashed out their feelings regarding their loss and ended the phone call sympathetic to each other's emotions.

Chapter 14

On March nineteenth, Lauren found herself standing in a courtroom confirming her presence during the docket call. Judy was with her and held her hand in support. After several cases were presented, the clerk called Lauren and Davin's cause number. Lauren didn't want to be there but had promised Davin she would follow through. She stood, walked to the bench, and respectfully addressed the judge. He asked a few questions, and Lauren answered. Without hesitation, he accepted their divorce for filing and dismissed her from the courtroom. In a haze, Lauren picked up her filed decree from the clerk's office. Afterward, she and Judy exited the courthouse and headed toward her car.

After starting it, Judy asked, "Are you okay?"

Lauren looked at her and replied, "Yeah. I think so." Lauren was a fighter. She had survived a lot of things and knew she would survive this too. Even though her marriage was over, she had hope for a healthier future.

Lauren's journey of healing continued. It was a tough one full of discomfort, frustration, tears, apologies, and forgiveness. In therapy, Lauren was able to acknowledge her shortcomings. She had made terrible decisions along her way. However, that did not make her a terrible person. Lauren had experienced an intense violation during her time in Iraq. Though she wasn't quite ready to work through it, she did recognize now that she and Davin were divorced there was no reason for her assault to remain a secret. Lauren had allowed the emotional pain associated with this event to consume her for far too long. Looking back, she realized her inability to deal with the attack created the catalyst for the detonation of her relationship with Davin. Her failures in its aftermath had almost destroyed her and for what? All that was left were pictures and souvenirs. Pieces of a life she and Davin shared. The ruined remains of a marriage she desperately wanted with a man she loved more than anything.

Lauren was heartbroken but thankful for the kindness and support of her family and friends. She was blessed to have people who stood by her during her fight for resolve and mental well-being. Without the distraction of Davin to impede her, Lauren trudged on in therapy. As she approached the date for her next psychological assessment, she knew it was time to report Lieutenant Renzo. He was a monster she'd inadvertently given power too, and she was ready to take it back.

On the day of her assessment, Lauren reported to her local Veteran's Administration Mental Health Building. She'd taken a few of these already and knew what questions were going to be asked. Lauren sat anxiously in the waiting room trying to maintain her courage. Finally, she was called. A nurse took her vitals and led her to the office of a waiting psychologist. Lauren sat down, and the psychologist proceeded to administer the assessment. She raced through the questions matter-of-factly as she checked off boxes. It was as if Lauren was just another service member on her conveyer belt of evaluations for the day. As she answered accordingly, Lauren began an internal struggle.

She was about to talk herself out of reporting the assault once again, when the psychologist asked, "Have you ever been the victim of an assault?"

When Lauren didn't promptly answer as she had before, the psychologist looked up at her and asked again, "Have you ever been the victim of an assault?"

There it is, thought Lauren. She had nothing more to lose. Davin had left her. At one time, she'd convinced herself it was better for them if Davin never knew, but that was over.

Lauren took a deep breath and hesitantly said, "Something bad happened to me." She was petrified about what would transpire next.

"Something happened to you," asked the psychologist. Lauren felt oddly freed and started to weep,

"Yes. Yes, it did. It happened in Iraq." Lauren could see the psychologist's demeanor change.

She put down her pen, handed Lauren a box of tissues, and inquired, "Were you sexually assaulted, Specialist Mayer?"

Lauren replied, "Yes. It was awful. I've never told anyone about it before." The psychologist picked up her phone and dialed a number.

Lauren listened as she spoke. "Hello, Mrs. Kinley. I have a veteran that needs to make a statement regarding a sexual trauma."

Lauren was nervous and began to worry. "Her name is Specialist Lauren Mayer. Can you see her right away?"

Lauren sat quietly as the psychologist thanked the other party and hung up the phone. Then she addressed Lauren. "Specialist, I need you to go to the VA in Fort Worth to make a statement. Go straight there. Do not stop."

Lauren realized the seriousness of her confession. None of it was under her control now. She'd jumped on a runaway train and had no other choice than to hang on for her life.

"Right now?" asked Lauren.

"Yes, ask for Mrs. Kinley when you get there. I'm calling her when you leave my office to let her know when to expect you," she said.

Lauren's heart was pounding with anxiety. It was time though. She was ready to rip off this band-aid and get it over with.

Lauren's mind was full of fear as she drove toward the VA hospital in Fort Worth. She followed her instructions and found Mrs. Kinley's office. Mrs. Kinley was a soft-spoken older woman. To ease Lauren's concern, she explained what would take place following her outcry. The first step was for Mrs. Kinley to record an informal statement. Lauren anxiously recounted her assault. Mrs. Kinley was patient and understanding while Lauren made her way through the painful details. Afterward, she gave Lauren an information packet as well as instructions to utilize when writing a full account. This would be her official statement.

Mrs. Kinley comforted Lauren by telling her, "I've done a lot of these. They never get easier. I do know from working with other survivors it's best to write your statement right away. Please don't wait. I'd like you to come back tomorrow." Lauren agreed to an appointment the next day and left to head to her parent's home since it was closer to Fort Worth than San Marcos.

Lauren called her mother while driving to Walnut Springs. She knew her mother wouldn't turn her away, but she still didn't want to show up unannounced. That evening Lauren sat down and wrote out a statement. Placing the details of her assault on paper and returning the statement to Mrs. Kinley for further investigation was almost as painful as the actual event itself. Although it was hard, Lauren was glad she'd finally done something about it. Weirdly, she felt like she'd set herself free from her monster's grasp.

In the coming months, she found herself feeling more whole than she had in a long time. In Iraq, her mission was that of a broadcast journalist. She was privileged to be a part of many stories.

Through therapy, Lauren realized she had a story of her own. It was a tough one that she sometimes hated, but it was hers. Over time, Lauren learned to embrace the person she'd become. She'd never be the young naive girl she'd started out as and she was okay with that. Her military service, her assault, her marriage to Davin, and her loss of their baby had all been tests of her fortitude, and she had survived.

This wouldn't be the end of her story, but it was a beginning to something new. She could proceed in her life without an awful secret. While nothing would ever happen to Lieutenant Renzo, it didn't matter. Lauren had taken her life back. Her courage to formally report him created an official documentation for her military record. It was a validation of her strength and a healing gift. One she wished she'd given herself a long time ago. While she'd closed several doors, she'd also opened a window of hope. Lauren set about living her life monster free. She found success in a new career, purchased a home, and eventually, she put Davin away in a box labeled Hendrix. When she missed him, as she often did, she'd pull him out of the closet to look at him. Lauren had saved all their letters, photos, and gifts from their life together. They were important reminders of sweet memories tangled with genuine regret. Lauren had rebuilt herself piece by piece, and it had been hard. At one time, Davin played a notable part in it all. Lauren earnestly tried to forget him, but she couldn't. She felt like she would always be in love him. Even though they'd gone separate ways, Lauren trusted their unique magnetism would one day pull them back together.

Late one evening years later, Lauren found herself smiling as she sat alone on her bedroom floor in the pair of beautiful shimmery brown pumps he'd bought her once upon a time.

She pulled one of Davin's letters from the box, unfolded it, and read, *"Lauren, Thank you so much for showing me what true love feels like. I hold our relationship close to my heart and spend the days dreaming of holding you in my arms again, hearing your laughter, and covering your body with kisses. I love you.*

Your, Shnuga Booga."

Lauren carefully folded it back before returning it along with the pumps to the box. A connection like the one they shared was rare. She sometimes wondered how often he thought of her. After all, they'd always agreed they were soul mates. Lauren placed the lid back on the box before sliding it onto the shelf in her closet. She paused in the open doorway for a moment. "I'll see you later, Shnuga," she said. Lauren laughed at herself and closed the door. Even though she had changed quite a bit, she was still the silly mess he'd fallen head over heels in love with, and Davin would always be the salty sailor who had stolen her heart and never returned it.

The End.